The Ronin Affair

The Ronin Affair

Adrianne Summer

To order additional copies of this book, contact:
Xlibris
1-888-795-4274
www.Xlibris.com
Orders@Xlibris.com
802621

To Sister Mary Clarence, who helped me get my act together.

Chapter 1

The car lock echoed in the parking garage. Reluctantly, Ronin began the long walk to the mall's French entrance.

It was his tenth wedding anniversary, and he was in no mood for romance. It'd only been a month since Ona burst into his office and confronted him. *"Are you sleeping with Alice?"* It wasn't so much a question as an accusation. She'd humiliated him, embarrassed his clients, and cost two of his colleagues their jobs.

Ona apologized, but he couldn't let it go. She was his wife, and she didn't trust him. Worse, she didn't respect him. All her apologies and assurances to the contrary had done little to change his mind or his heart. But tonight, considering the significance of the occasion, he'd decided to call and end the hostilities.

*****

A chime sounded as Ronin came through the door.

"Good afternoon. Welcome to Amour et Chocolat. May I help you find you something?" Solis greeted him.

Ronin didn't acknowledge her. He skipped the counter and made his way past the marble-topped tasting tables to the mahogany display cases with prepackaged specialty items. Amour et Chocolat imported confections from around the world, and they were the only confectioner that carried the French truffles Ona loved.

"Damn it," Ronin murmured under his breath. He couldn't remember which truffles Ona liked, and the boxes went on forever.

Solis smiled to herself. Ronin's frenzied search for prepackaged chocolates told her all she needed to know. She called to him from behind the counter.

"If you bring that run-of-the-mill box of chocolates home, you'll be in the doghouse for sure."

Ronin turned to the voice behind the counter, prepared to tell her to mind her own business, until he came face-to-face with her soft brown eyes, warm copper skin, and devastating smile.

"Is it that obvious?" Ronin replied, ending his fruitless search for the right box of truffles.

"Those boxes say, 'Honey, I forgot, so at the last minute, I dropped by the store and got these.'"

"Don't spare a brothas feelings." Ronin clutched his chest, feigning injury.

Solis's eyes sparkled with amusement. "I can help, but it's going to cost you."

"A gentleman never refuses a lady. You got me. How much?"

"A few hundred, give or take."

"Seriously?"

Solis raised her left hand— "Doghouse?"—and then her right— "Or . . ."

"I'll take the door on the right."

"You've chosen wisely. Birthday or anniversary? Dinner or night in?"

"Tenth anniversary, dinner out."

"A milestone. Inga's Garden is two blocks down Main Street. Ask for the doghouse bouquet with yellow roses. Smirnov Jewelers is on Fifth Street. Get a diamond and birthstone pendant. That way, you don't have to worry about sizing. Ask for the silver box. While you're gone, I'll hand pack you a box of our best truffles—you know, the ones she likes that you can't remember." Solis winked.

"How do you know all of this?"

"Trade secrets," she replied coyly.

"Solis?" Ronin pointed to her name tag. "Do you offer advice often?"

"I usually don't have to. Most patrons ask for it, Mr. . . .?"

"Ronin Jackson. Please call me Ronin. Well, Solis, you've given me some errands to run. See you in a few."

"I'll be waiting." Solis waved him away.

Ronin glanced over his shoulder as he exited the store. *What twisted irony put a temptation like you in a candy store?* Ronin rolled his eyes at the thought, turning his wrist to check the time. *Door number 2.*

****

Piper smiled at Ronin on his way out of the store. "Solis! He was in here?"

"Yes, he came for an anniversary gift. I sent him on a few errands to make it special."

"Why are all the hot ones taken? And why do they only come into the store when you're here? Don't answer that, you goddamn Egyptian goddess." Piper pouted.

Piper, twenty-five, was forever on the hunt for Mr. Wrong. A pretty blonde, with sapphire blue eyes and porcelain skin, she got her fair share of attention.

"Piper, this is a candy boutique. Men only come in here when they need something for another woman. Mother, daughter, wife . . . doesn't matter. If you want to find a single guy, you need to work in the outlets. Tons of eligible bachelors coming in and out of there."

"Nah, too many teenagers. Teenagers are a pain in the ass."

"Oh, so I'm a pain in the ass?"

"Solis, you couldn't be a teenager if you tried. You don't know how. I didn't have my shit together at your age."

"You don't have your shit together now." Solis nudged her playfully.

"Very funny. Marlon will be happy, you'll put us over quota with just that one box."

"What does Marlon say, 'If you want a man to buy something . . . have a beautiful woman sell it to him.'"

"And that doesn't sound even remotely sexists to you? I know he's your cousin, but he's the manager too."

Solis set a sateen candy box on the counter. "Sexist? No. Ingenious? Definitely. You gotta know your clientele. It's all a show. Piper, you are the slightly unattainable girl next door. Bobby is the All-American boy you'd find in any Gap ad. There's a reason we're the highest-grossing boutique. It's also why we get paid so well."

"Still sexist, but it beats commission. You want me to help you with that box?"

"No. I got it."

"I'll be in the back. Holler when tall-dark-and-yummy comes back. He may not be Mr. Right, but I could settle for Mr. Right Now."

Tall, dark, and yummy—a good description. Broad-shouldered, with rich umber skin, a high fade, and a close-cut goatee in a fitted Armani suit, Ronin was an ebony daydream.

Solis sighed. "Why are all the good ones taken? No, Piper, why are all the good ones older than me?"

Chapter 2

Ronin held the door for another patron and followed her inside. Life in the Jackson home was better of late. His anniversary gifts and after-dinner sex calmed the waters. Ona was happier, but he was restless, distracted.

It was Solis. Their brief encounter the month before had a profound effect on him.

The boutique was busy. Ronin perused the shelves, waiting for Solis to notice him. Conflicted, he half hoped she wouldn't but was elated when she did.

"Ronin! Welcome back. I take it your gifts were a hit?"

"Door number 2, definitely the right choice. Thank you."

"My pleasure. So, you're back for more . . . chocolate?" Solis blushed. *Seriously, Solis, could you be more obvious?*

Solis' timid but less than subtle flirtation caught Ronin off guard. It'd been a while since a woman played coquet with him. Encouraged, he decided to up the ante.

"I was wondering if I could take you for coffee, you know, to say thank you for all your help."

"Today? I don't get off for another hour."

Ronin grabbed a bag of chocolate-covered almonds. "If that's a yes, I'll wait."

Solis shot him a wickedly playful look. "You said you weren't here to buy chocolate."

Ronin grinned. "What kind of customer would I be if I didn't? I'll see you in an hour. Café Paris, okay?"

"Café Paris? I'm a little underdressed, but okay."

"Great. I'll be outside."

*****

Ronin Jackson was the sexy kind of charming; that was hard to forget. She'd often wondered if she'd see him again. Until now, it'd been nothing more than a harmless fantasy.

Solis checked her reflection in the breakroom mirror; as always, echoes of her mother stared back at her. She unpinned her hair, letting it fall past her shoulders. She rolled down her sleeves and opened a few buttons on her shirt. For a finishing touch, she glossed her lips and freshened her perfume. Satisfied, she headed for the exit. Ronin was waiting right where he said he'd be.

What are you doing, Solis? He's a man—a married man. Solis stood still, paused by the scolding of her conscience.

Because of her uncommon beauty, older men hit on her all the time. The perverts, the persistent, and the predators—Solis knew them all too well. But Ronin, Ronin didn't feel like the others. Solis dismissed her conscience and went out to meet him.

"Best a girl could do in five minutes," Solis shrugged, commenting on her appearance.

"You did a lot in five minutes. Not that you needed it."

"Flattery will get you everywhere. Shall we?"

"After you."

Chapter 3

"*Bienvenue au Café Paris*. How may we have the pleasure of serving you today?"

"Thank you. Two, please. On the terrace," Ronin replied.

"Yes, sir. Will you and the beautiful lady follow me?"

Patrons in business attire conversed cheerfully over coffee. Servers moved quickly from kitchen to table and back again, never forgetting to smile. White linen and silver place settings dressed every table. A sky light gave the very convincing illusion of being outside on a warm sunny Paris day. On the terrace, one could people-watch while sipping their noisette, perched above the mall patrons one floor below. Café Paris was as far from a Starbucks as one could get.

"Here we are." The host pulled out the chair for Solis.

"Thank you, Lucas."

"You remember me?" Lucas asked, surprised.

"Yes. Did your mother like the Brazilian chocolates?"

"She said they were sinfully delicious! Your box was so lovely, she kept it. Thank you. Your server will be with you momentarily."

Ronin waited for Lucas to leave before he spoke. "He likes you."

"Who? Lucas? No. It's the name. People like it when you remember their names, their moments. It makes them feel valued, important."

"How long have you worked at the boutique?"

"A year. I worked for Ms. Inga before I worked here. She and her husband Mr. Smirnov own the florist and the jewelry store."

"I hope you get commission. You're very good at what you do."

"You're sweet."

"I'm a contract lawyer. I practice at Jackson & Owens. Our offices are on the fourth floor. I can't believe you've worked here for a year and I've never seen you."

"I'm not always here. I think that's our server."

"My name is Julie. Have we decided? Would you care for a list? We have a variety of specialty coffees and an assortment of macarons."

"Julie, I'd like a *noisette Vanille crème d'amande.*"

Julie noted Solis' order and turned to Ronin. "And you, sir?"

"Just coffee with cream."

"Coffee?" Solis asked incredulously. "You don't come to Café Paris and order *café Americain.* Julie, he'll have a *café aux noisettes à la crème.* Thank you."

"Good choice. Be back soon." Julie left for the kitchen.

Ronin cocked an eyebrow. "You speak French, or you've been here before?"

"*Oui, je parle français.* I came here once on an assignment for a French class."

"You're a student. Where?"

"I start my junior year at Roosevelt High in the fall."

Ronin sat quietly as the weight of her words sunk in. He couldn't believe it. Solis carried herself with an intelligence and maturity far beyond her years. It didn't matter. The voice of reason was clear. He needed to leave.

"Oh, you thought . . . sixteen. I'll be seventeen in December. I'm sorry. You didn't ask. I should've said something. I won't be upset if you want to go."

Julie returned. "I have a *café aux noisettes à la crème* for the gentleman, and for the lady with impeccable taste, I have a *noisette vanille crème d'amande.* Is there anything else I can get for you?"

Solis gave Julie a smile and a nod. "No, thank you."

"You're welcome. I'll be back to check on you in a while." Julie made a hasty retreat toward the barista counter.

"We could ask her to make these to go," Solis offered.

"I asked you to coffee to thank you. What kind of thank-you would it be if I left before you got to enjoy it?"

"You do this often?" Solis asked in earnest.

"No. I'm not in the habit of asking beautiful young women who are not my wife out for coffee."

"Then I guess I better enjoy it."

Solis sipped her coffee slowly, checking the temperature. Ronin did the same.

"Mmm, now that's good. You'll have to tell me what it is in English so I can order it again."

"Hazelnut coffee with almond cream. Glad you like it."

"Speaking of, Ona loved everything. But why yellow roses?" Ronin asked.

"Red roses say, 'I went to the florist and spent a lot of money.' Yellow roses say, 'I went to the florist and picked out something special just for you.' Big difference. Don't take this the wrong way, but after ten years of marriage, I'd like to think a man would have it together."

Ronin laughed. "Brutal, beautiful, and brilliant—a triple threat."

"I tend to be too honest. I'm sorry."

"Don't be. I find it refreshing. Sometimes the years, the kids, work . . . life, you just drop the ball."

"Well, I'm glad I was able to help you pick it up. You have kids?"

"Two sons: Ronin Jr., ten, and Robert, six."

"Sounds fun. I bet they're sweet."

"They are. And you?"

Solis felt her phone vibrate. "Ronin, I have to go. Thank you for this. I really enjoyed it."

Solis left the table too quickly for Ronin to stand. He watched from the terrace as she exited the café.

Waves of coffee broke on the sides of his cup when his silent ringer went off. It was Ona. He'd ignored her last text, he figured he better answer.

"Hey, sweetness. I'm sorry. Lunch with a client ran long. I'm on my way home now. Do you need me to stop and get anything?"

"No. I was worried. You didn't text me back," Ona replied.

"Sorry, my phone was on silent. See you soon."

Ronin hung up. For the first time in ten years, he'd lied to his wife about where he'd been and who he'd been with. He found his lack of emotion around the act unsettling. *What is wrong with you?*

Before he could call for it, Lucas appeared with the check. He set it on the table, giving Ronin the oddest look.

"For you, sir, when you're ready. No rush."

Lucas turned on his heels, back to the host area. Ronin opened the billfold, and a pink monogramed note card fell out.

"Thank you. Solis Monroe. 530—"

Ronin ran his fingers over the card. Solis intrigued him in a way no woman ever had. It was easy to forget she was sixteen—too easy. *Throw it away. You've indulged this long enough. You shouldn't be here.*

Ronin tucked Solis' number away in his wallet.

Chapter 4

"Ronin, where are you?" Ona asked. "We're supposed to be at Joi and Marcus's this afternoon, remember? The boys and I are here waiting for you."

"How could I forget?"

"Ronin, she's my sister. Marcus is a great guy. I know you like him."

"I'm meeting up with Damien to go over legal briefs."

"Maybe Damien can come. The boys would love to see their uncle."

"I'll ask Damien to come and meet you and the boys over there later. Okay?"

"Later? What—"

"Love you . . . I gotta go."

Dial tone. Ronin hung up before she could get the words out. *What's going on with him?*

Ona relaxed in the shade of the patio while the boys played in the shallow end of the pool. Ona had no intention of getting in the water. A statuesque five feet eleven inches, with flawless blue brown skin, striking eyes, and an eye-catching figure, her fuchsia Gucci bikini was about fashion, not function. Thankfully, Marcus was on duty as both referee and lifeguard.

Joi sat down on a chaise next to Ona. "Look at those boys. A bunch of guppies, all of them. We're never going to get them out of the pool."

Ona half smiled but didn't respond.

"Earth to Ona?" Joi waved her hand in front of Ona's face.

"Sorry, sis."

"Are you going to tell me what's on your mind?"

"Ronin."

"Where's Ronin anyway? Trying to avoid me?" Joi snorted.

"He's with Damien. He'll be over later."

"Damien knows he's fine with those dreamy eyes. You should've married Damien." Joi smiled deviously.

"Have you no shame, Joi?"

"None. Come on. What's up?"

"Ronin has been distant lately. It's like the closer I try to get to him, the farther away he gets."

Joi peered over her Dolce & Gabbana sunglasses. "You know that's how it starts."

"Don't go there, Joi. What was I thinking, going to his office like that? He still hasn't forgiven me."

"All the signs were there. Who knew it was Brodie?"

"I still can't believe Brodie left you for Alice Stubbs."

"I wasn't around. She was. It doesn't make it right, but it is what it is. I'm just grateful she cares for Little Brodie and Michael. I'd never tell the home-wrecking bitch that, but it's true."

"Mom was around. That didn't stop Dad from leaving her—leaving us."

"That was a long time ago, Ona. Have you talked to Ronin?"

"I've tried. It's infuriating."

"Finish that glass and have another. I find life looks a lot better when seen through a bottle of wine or two."

Ona drained her glass and offered it to Joi for another pour. She peered through the stemware mockingly as if expecting her life to be better. The thought of Ronin leaving conjured a toxic brew of fear, rage, and desperation inside her no glass of wine could fix. She wasn't her mother or her sister. She wasn't going to let what happened to them happen to her.

****

Irritated and running late. Ronin called Damien from the mall entrance.

"D, I need you to come with me to Joi's house for a barbecue today, and if Ona asks, I was with you all afternoon."

"Ro, I got plans."

"Whoever she is, bring her with you or bow out. I'm sure you can think of something."

"Wait, why do you need me to tell Ona you're with me?"

"Stop giving me shit and just do it, okay?" Ronin pleaded.

"Fine, what time?"

"About two."

"Hold up. It's twelve. What are you? I can't believe it. Who is she?"

"There's no she. You know I'd rather chew lead than spend one minute with Joi Cooper; and the thought of spending the whole afternoon talking to Marcus makes my head hurt."

"Then don't go."

"Be real, you know I have to. She's Ona sister, the two are inseparable."

"And this is why I don't have a wife. You're really not going to tell me who she is?"

It was no surprise to Ronin that Damien would find the idea of his infidelity amusing. The only thing Damien studied in college more than the law was beautiful women. He had no intention of getting married. To him, monogamy was a disease that made men weak, and he avoided it like the plague.

"There is no she. I got to go."

"Be careful. You ain't got the skills to keep two women happy, and Ona is crazy as hell."

"Yeah. Yeah. Bye."

Ronin joined Solis at a table outside the café. He stopped a barista. "Espresso, please."

Solis could tell he wasn't himself when he sat down. "Ronin, is everything okay?"

"Sorry I'm late. Ona's upset. I didn't stay and go to a barbecue at her sister's house. I told her I'd come later."

"You could've gone. I'd have understood."

Ronin gently touched her cheek. "And miss our weekly date?"

Smiling, the barista set the espresso on the table between them.

"I love our dates too, but I'm not naïve. You're a married man with responsibilities."

"Solis Monroe, how are you sixteen?"

"I get that question all the time. But seriously, get a babysitter. Take her out. Make it something simple."

"You want me to spend time with her?"

Ronin couldn't believe it. Solis was encouraging him to spend more time with his wife. It was sound advice, but coming from her, he couldn't help but wonder if her feelings for him were mutual.

"Ronin, she's your wife."

"Yes. She is. A date night? It's doable. My parents are out of town . . . my assistant, maybe she knows a good sitter."

"I'm off Friday. I'll do it. I love kids."

"And how do you suppose I explain that I just happened to find a charming and lovely babysitter?"

"You're a lawyer. Isn't that what you guys do?" Solis winked at him playfully.

"It's been a while since I argued a case, but I think I can come up with a convincing argument. Friday night?"

"Friday night it is. Ona should give Dahlia a call."

"Dahlia?"

"My mother."

It always caught him off guard when Solis referred to her mother as Dahlia. There was something there, but he wasn't ready to ask, and she wasn't ready to share.

Solis wrote Dahlia's phone number on one of her monogramed cards and handed it to Ronin. "Have Ona call tomorrow. It'll give you a little time to make your case, counselor. I got to get back. See you Friday."

Solis left the table. A young man stopped her. She smiled sweetly at him. Ronin couldn't hear what she said, but it was clear she shot him down. The man ran to catch up with his friend. Ronin listened to their conversation as they walked by.

"Did you see her? Damn, that kind of sexy should be against the law." The younger of the men shook his head.

"It is against the law. You hit that, and you'll be wearing bracelets and a jumpsuit," his friend replied.

Bracelets and orange jumpsuits weren't the half of it. He was committing suicide. Solis could cost him everything. And now, now he was bringing her home. Ronin dropped cash on table and headed for the exit. Deep in thought, Ona's call startled him. *What now?*

"Hey, beautiful," Ronin answered.

"Ronin get over here quick. Marcus wants to start the grill. You know what happened last time," Ona whispered.

"Roger that. Get the fire extinguisher. Hide the matches. "I'm on my way. Be there in twenty. Oh, Damien is coming too."

"Already done," Ona chuckled. "Great! The boys will be happy. Love you. Hurry up."

"Love you too."

Ronin synched his Bluetooth to the car and dialed Damien. The line rang longer than he expected. He was about to hang up and dial again when Damien answered.

"You owe me! Bailing on Aaliyah got me mad shit."

"You'll smooth it over." Ronin chuckled. "Meet me over there in thirty."

"If Ona asks, what were we doing all afternoon?"

"I told her we were going over legal briefs."

"Working? Ro, we got to work on your alibi skills if you're going to keep this up. Is she worth it?"

"D, the last time, there's no she."

"You're a terrible liar. See you at Joi's."

Damien was right, he did need a new alibi. Ona was suspicious by nature, and two months of working on Saturdays wouldn't go unnoticed for long.

****

Solis giggled. She couldn't help it. Ronin made her deliriously happy. He didn't treat her like a child. He listened when she talked and had a genuine interest in what she had to say. The attraction between them was palpable, but Ronin never once made her feel uncomfortable. Other than a kiss on the hand or cheek, he'd barely touched her.

Marlon was waiting at the counter when she returned. "Hey, cousin. Where you been?" Marlon asked.

"Eating lunch. That's usually what people do at lunchtime," Solis quipped.

"Don't play dumb. You came in here like a cat who'd caught a mouse. Who is he? Where'd you meet him?"

"You checking up on me?"

"Maybe. Don't change the subject."

"His name is Ronin. I helped him with a last-minute anniversary gift. The coffee was a thank-you."

"Not tall, dark, and yummy? I'm so jelly." Piper sighed.

"Thank you, Piper." Solis glared at her.

"Coffee? How helpful were you?"

"I sent him to see Inga and Demetri and packed him a specialty box of truffles. That helpful, jerk!"

"Nah, that ain't it. He wants something. How old is he?"

Marlon asked the one question Solis didn't want to answer. Marlon could change roles at the drop of a hat. If he decided to play the overprotective brother, he'd tell Dahlia and put an end to Ronin with a quickness. Solis knew she had to tread lightly.

"I don't know . . . thirty something, but it isn't what you think."

"The hell it ain't! I hired you to keep you out of trouble and help you earn some money while going to school. Don't make me regret it."

"Whatever, Marlon! You hired me because I'm the best damn employee you have. I bring in more repeat business than anyone, including you, cousin."

"Sass all you want. I'm serious."

"I'll prove it. Ronin and Ona asked me to babysit for them next Friday night. He gave me his card with his wife's number and their address on it. He wants me to have Dahlia call her tomorrow to make sure it's okay. See?"

Solis took Ronin's card out of her pocket and showed it to him. Marlon gave the card a once-over and handed it back.

"We'll see. I'll be in the office."

Solis joined Piper behind the counter. "Really, Piper? Could you be any less helpful?"

"Jailbait," Piper whispered.

"Not funny, Piper."

"Oh, but it is. Liar," she laughed.

"Don't you have something to do?" Solis asked, irritated.

"No, but you do. Enjoy." Piper sauntered off.

Piper was joking around; but the situation was serious. Marlon knew her better than anyone, and it was only a matter of time before he figured it out.

Chapter 5

Dahlia leaned over the steering wheel. "These houses are so big; you can't see the numbers."

"Twenty-seven. It should be up there on the right," Solis pointed.

Dahlia pulled into the drive and cut the engine. Solis got out, motioning for Dahlia to follow. She didn't.

"Solis, why do you want me to come to these people's door?"

Solis knew Dahlia didn't do well in new social situations, especially ones where she felt inferior. She had to cajole, convince, and finally, drag Dahlia into the car to get her here.

"Dahlia, the Jacksons are people, no different than you and me. Chill out. It'd be weird if you didn't come to the door and meet them."

"Look around. If you think for one minute there ain't no difference between us and them, you're fooling yourself."

Dahlia had a point. Ronin lived in The Willows, a gated community of modern colonials with sweeping driveways and tree-lined streets; it was hard to believe they were only twenty minutes from their home in Laurel Heights. It didn't matter. She needed Dahlia to come to the door.

Solis came around to the driver side door and opened it. "Whatever, Dahlia! Just come already!"

"Fine." Dahlia got out of the car.

****

Ona greeted them at the door. She and Dahlia exchanged pleasantries. Ona explained they would be back late and asked if it was okay for Ronin to take Solis home. Dahlia readily agreed and left.

"Okay, a quick tour." Ona gestured for Solis to follow.

They walked past the grand staircase through the living room into the family room.

"This is the only place outside of their rooms where the boys can play and watch TV. Through here is the kitchen. You may help yourself to anything. Our emergency contacts and instructions for the night are on the fridge. Don't let the boys eat too late. The bathroom is just down the hall here."

Solis could tell Ona took pride in her décor. It was a beautiful home. But no one would guess a family with young children lived in it. And the house didn't feel like Ronin at all.

"Mrs. Jackson, you have a lovely home."

"Call me Ona. Thank you for watching the boys and for my anniversary gifts."

"He told you?" Solis asked, surprised and alarmed.

"I figured it out. Ronin would never have picked yellow roses or the right truffles. I knew there had to a woman involved. I'm just glad it was you." Ona smiled.

Ronin came downstairs, interrupting their conversation.

"Solis, thanks for coming. I hope you and your mom didn't have trouble finding the place."

"Just a little," Solis replied, trying not to make direct eye contact. She had a terrible poker face and didn't want Ona getting any ideas.

Ronin called up the stairs. "Boys, come and meet Solis. She's going to watch you tonight while Mommy and Daddy go out."

Ronin Jr. and Robert thundered down the staircase.

"Hi, Solis. I'm Robert. How old are you?"

Solis smiled and knelt to Robert's level. "Well, Robert, you're six, and I'm ten years older than you. Can you guess how old I am?"

"Sixteen," Ronin Jr. answered.

"Right. Ronin, you look just like your father. Is that why they call you Little Ronin?"

"I guess so." He shrugged.

"What do you boys want to do first? Maybe a movie? I brought my favorite microwave kettle corn."

"Popcorn!" Robert squealed, running off to the kitchen.

"You're really pretty. Do you have a boyfriend?" Ronin Jr. asked sheepishly.

"Ronin! Go find your brother," Ona snapped.

Ronin Jr. dropped his head and turned to leave. Solis could tell Ona's reaction embarrassed him.

"Ronin. If I met boys like you, I'd have a boyfriend for sure," Solis winked.

He smiled and hurried off.

"I got this. You two should get going."

"Yes, let's go, Ona." Ronin grabbed their coats from the closet.

"Solis, are you sure you don't have any questions? You can call if you need anything at all. Anything."

"Ona, for god's sake, I think Solis can handle it." Ronin pushed her out the door.

Solis shut the door behind them, thankful they were gone and prayerful their interaction was brief enough as not to give Ona any ideas. Solis could tell from Ona's comments about the gifts; it wouldn't take much for her to start jumping to conclusions.

"Solis, can we make the popcorn now?" Robert stood in the hallway waiting, albeit impatiently.

"Yes. Right behind you."

****

Ronin settled into the drive, Ona beside him. He could tell something was on her mind. Against his better judgment and at risk of undoing all his work, he waded into the tepid waters between them.

"Hey, we can't let the boys have a better night than us." Ronin nudged her.

"Sorry, love. Solis is sweet. The boys took to her."

"I'm glad you like her."

"Her mother seems a little off."

"How so?"

"She hardly asked any questions when I spoke with her about Solis sitting with the boys, and she left without staying to meet you. Who does that?"

"Maybe she just isn't a helicopter parent. Solis is sixteen."

"I'm not a helicopter parent. I just like to know what's going on in my sons' lives."

"And you do. You're a great mom."

"Thank you, love."

"What are we going to see?"

"Something foreign."

"Foreign it is."

Solis never spoke about her family in any detail. From what he could tell, Marlon was the closest thing Solis had to a father, and she adored him. It bothered him. How had this twenty-year-old kid become the man responsible for Solis's well-being? Where the hell was her father? Where was Dahlia? The questions weren't new. He'd had them from the beginning.

Chapter 6

"That's my house on the left," Solis pointed.

Ronin stopped the car across the street and turned in his seat to face her. "I thought about you a lot tonight."

"Really? I hope Ona didn't notice. She doesn't trust you."

"How do you know that?"

"You gave her three beautiful gifts. She didn't act pleasantly surprised by your thoughtfulness. Instead, she thought you had help— female help. Not to mention she constantly text or calls you whenever you're away."

"You got all that from just meeting her the one time?"

"She doesn't hide it, at least not well. 'I'm glad it was you.' Clearly, a warning. She knew you could hear her. Your unhappiness, the bitterness and resentment you keep just beneath the surface, I understand it now."

Ronin was speechless. Solis read him like a book. She had from the day they met.

"I'm sorry, Ronin, I shouldn't have said anything. It isn't my place to—"

"Solis, what am I to you?"

"You're my friend," Solis replied quietly.

"Solis, I'm thirty-nine, a little old to be your friend."

"Okay. What am I to you? Your friend? Or your Ona antidote?"

"Aw, there it is . . . that brutal beauty. Come here."

Solis leaned toward him. Ronin placed a hand on either side of her face and gently kissed her. "You are my friend. Do you trust me, Solis?"

"Can we talk tomorrow?" Solis asked, nervously avoiding the question.

"Yes. What time?"

"Eleven. Meet me at Witt Creek Park on the benches across from the pond."

Ronin kissed her hand. "Until tomorrow, friend."

Solis giggled. "Go home, Ronin."

"I will when you're inside. Good night."

"Good night."

Solis hurried to the door. She waved to let Ronin know it was okay to leave. She was fumbling with her keys when Marlon opened the door.

"You dirty little liar."

"Damn it, Marlon! You scared the shit out of me! Why are you up anyway?" Solis asked, closing the door.

"When I got home, I checked in on you. You weren't in your room."

"I had a babysitting gig, remember? Two of the cutest little boys—"

"Babysitting my ass. You lied to me. You never lie to me."

"What are you talking about? I was absolutely babysitting. You can even ask Dahlia. She dropped me off, came in, met the family, and everything."

"So why were you in the car so long?"

"Are you spying on me? Seriously?"

"I don't have to spy. You were right outside the damn house! 'It isn't like that, Marlon. It's just a babysitting thing, Marlon.' Solis, you've never even kissed a boy before, and here you are with a grown man!"

"I'm sixteen, not ten, Marlon!"

"How long has this been going on, and why didn't you tell me?"

"There's nothing to tell."

"Are you sleeping him?"

"Marlon!"

"Don't Marlon me! Somebody has to keep after you. God knows Dahlia ain't." Marlon sighed.

"I'm still a virgin, not that it's any of your business."

"You made it my business when you didn't tell me about it from jump."

"Ugh, I hate you sometimes! I'm not working tomorrow! And no, I'm not asking permission! Find someone to cover me!" Solis stormed to her room and slammed the door.

Marlon laughed. "Door slamming. Definitely sixteen, not ten."

Solis' reaction confirmed his suspicions. There was a man in her life, and his name was Ronin Jackson. He wasn't worried, just pissed she didn't tell him. He'd taught her well. If this Ronin Jackson were dangerous, she'd know. Just in case, he'd keep a closer eye, inquire about her comings and goings more. She'd hate it, but he wouldn't give her choice.

*****

The drive from Laurel Heights back to The Willows felt like forever. Solis weighed heavy on his mind and his body. He didn't get out of the car right away, choosing instead to savor the waning hints of her perfume and the softness of her lips. He felt himself grow thick with need. Closing his eyes, he willed his body into submission and got out of the car.

Ona met him at the door when he came in.

"You got Solis home okay? She did a marvelous job with the boys. We should have her back. Maybe we could make Friday our regular date night? What do you think?"

Ronin grabbed Ona, pulling her to the floor. He swallowed her mouth with his and tore her panties from between her legs. He took her with a hard and deliberate strike, chasing release. Ona cried out. He drove deeper, harder; stifling her pleas and moans with brutal kisses. Ronin felt her orgasm crest and let his wash over him with a primal growl. He rolled off, coming to rest beside her.

"What's gotten into you?" Ona asked, bewildered.

"You're right. We should have a regular date night," Ronin replied breathless.

"If this is what I can expect to get out of them, then yeah!" Ona picked up the remnants of her clothing. "You think we could do that again? Maybe a little slower this time?"

"Slower this time. I've got to work tomorrow afternoon. I'll be gone an hour or two."

"No problem. The boys and I can find something to get into. See you upstairs."

Ona wanted him. He should be ecstatic. He wasn't. He wanted Solis. From the moment she came into his life, she was all he wanted. She was too young. He would have to wait.

Chapter 7

Witt Creek Park was one of the nicest and most secluded in Denton, the perfect place for a midday rendezvous.

Sunlight danced in and out of the shade as the trees rustled in the wind. The park was empty, save a few would be fishermen casting their lines in the water. Ronin and Solis kept to themselves as they made their way around the pond.

Ronin could sense Solis' unease. The light in her eyes was dim, the song of her smile silent. Ronin placed her hand in his, closing the distance between them. When she didn't pull away, he felt it was safe to talk.

"Solis, last night . . . I haven't asked you about a lot of things. I hoped in time you'd trust—"

"Ask me anything," Solis cut him off.

"You never talk about your mom, your dad, or anybody in your family, except Marlon."

"I don't have a lot of family. It's just me, Dahlia, and Marlon."

"Why do you call your mother Dahlia?"

"Dahlia tries, but mothering isn't really her thing. She was fourteen when she had me. It's hard to be a mother that young. People judge you. If people think you have a little sister, not so much. I've never met my father. He's been in jail my entire life."

"Do you know what happened?"

"Darrell. Dahlia doesn't talk about him. My grandmother blames Dahlia for him being in jail. They used to fight about it a lot."

"Your grandmother? I thought it was just the three of you?"

"Ulayla Monroe. I'm grateful she took my mother in and saved Marlon from foster care. If she hadn't, God only knows what would've happened to us. That said, her charity came with a lot of emotional abuse. Dahlia and Marlon got the worst of it."

"Why would she take you guys in and then treat you like that?"

"I think she took us in out of obligation. What else do you do when your daughter is a drug-addicted prostitute and your son is a felon doing life? I think it was hard for her having us around as reminders."

"Ulayla took your mother in? Where was her mother?"

"Strung out, in and out of jail. Apparently, that was Darrell's fault too, but I'm not sure. I don't know the whole story, only bits and pieces. Dahlia never talks about her either. I met Marie once. But I was young, so it's hard to remember. I have her name, Solis Marie."

Ronin was horrified. He struggled to hide his shock. *You're that guy. You're that asshole taking advantage of a girl with . . .*

Solis stopped abruptly. "You're thinking you're that guy? You aren't. And I'm not that girl. Don't think that. Don't change how you think of me. This is why I didn't tell you—why I don't tell anyone!"

"Solis, I don't think—"

"Don't lie to me. I can see it on your face."

The panic in Solis' voice was real. She'd trusted him. He needed to pull it together.

"It's okay, Solis. None of this changes anything. I swear it. Say you believe me." Ronin watched as the fear in her eyes gave way to a smile.

"I believe you."

He still had questions but could see it was best to let it go for now and change the subject.

"Good. Sit down." Ronin sat on the nearest bench, motioning for Solis to follow. "I have something for you. Here." Ronin handed her a hundred dollars.

"What's this?" Solis asked, surprised.

"For watching the boys last night."

"I told you I'd do it for free."

"I'm not going to let you. We're having a party at the house next Saturday evening. A few of our colleagues, their spouses, maybe a few friends. Do you think you could watch the boys that evening?"

"The party, is it business or pleasure?"

"Both. Fundraising dinner for Ona's nonprofit, Maya's Library. It provides grants for libraries at underfunded schools."

"I've heard of it. Ona runs it? That's amazing! They funded the computer lab at Roosevelt."

"Yeah, Ona is a master fundraiser. She's always on the hunt for new donors. I offer my clients up as tribute and provide free legal services."

"The fundraising Hunger Games?" Solis laughed.

"You haven't seen Ona pry open the hands of the reluctant."

"Ona is okay with this?"

"I spend a lot of time entertaining clients. Some wise young sage suggested I spend more time with my wife. Figured I could kill two birds with one stone if I entertained the clients at home."

"I admire a man who can take suggestions. But are you sure Ona is good with this?"

"It was her idea. We'd like you to babysit for us every Friday night you're available. She's going to call you and Dahlia today to talk about it."

"Sex must've been good when you got home. No woman as jealous as Ona is going to let her guard down like that unless she's in a very good mood."

Ronin's laugh was deep and satisfying. "Solis Monroe, you kill me. I've been known to curl a toe or two, but I wasn't thinking about her. You know that, right?"

"Ronin, you don't have to worry about things like that with me. I'm not the jealous type. She's your wife."

"Most women wouldn't see things that way."

"I'm not most women."

"No. No you are not." Ronin lifted her chin and kissed her. He longed to make the kiss deeper, but they weren't alone. He placed his hand over her heart. "There is more in here than you know, Solis Monroe. Maybe one day you'll let me show you."

Solis blushed. "One day. Are you sure this is what you want? Ona and I under the same roof for a whole evening?"

"Yes. I'm good."

"Well then, I'll see you Saturday." Solis stood.

"You in a hurry?"

"No, but you should be. Ona has text you at least three times in the last thirty minutes."

"Let me take you home."

Solis kissed him on the cheek. "Nope. Your wife is waiting. I'll see you Saturday."

Ronin watched Solis walk away. When she was safely on her bus, he reclined on the bench and checked his phone.

Ona was calling—again. He sent her to voice mail. He wasn't ready to talk to her, to anyone. He needed time to process the ton of bricks Solis laid on him. She was afraid he'd think less of her, but nothing could be further from the truth. Her brokenness only made her more beautiful.

His inner compass of right and wrong tried to move him, but his heart silenced the notion for good. Life without Solis was no longer an option.

Chapter 8

Solis served herself and joined Marlon at the kitchen table. She tried to ignore his inquisitive grin but, in the end, gave in. "What, Marlon?"

"Was your afternoon . . . delightful?" Marlon gleefully turned the spaghetti with his spoon.

"Not in the way you're suggesting."

Marlon frowned. "He's either got an iron will, a limp dick, or he's a pussy. Which is it?"

"Maybe he's just a gentleman."

"He's a pussy. Definitely a pussy."

"What would you know about pussy?" Solis smirked.

"Touché. But I knew how to get it done back in my closet days. The ladies loved me." Marlon laughed, stuffing a fork full of spaghetti in his mouth.

If Solis was an Egyptian goddess, then Marlon was a god. Six-three with light eyes, warm mocha skin, and a linebacker's build, Marlon attracted women in droves. Ironically, that was his problem. Being surrounded by women all the time gave everyone the impression he was straight. Many a woman was disappointed when they found out Marlon was playing for the other team.

"You are a sick and twisted individual, Marlon Jones."

"You have no idea. Find out if the brother has any rich friends, a brother on the down low."

Solis rolled her eyes. "I'll get right on that. You're going to hate me, but I need next Saturday off, and I may not be able to work every Friday night. Ronin and Ona have asked me to babysit for them."

"I'm scared of you, all hand that rocks the cradle and shit. He's a pussy and crazy. You sure know how to pick 'em."

"Shut up, Marlon. Seriously."

"Okay. It'll suck, but that may help me out. Bobby and Piper have been asking for more hours."

Dahlia came in the kitchen and joined them at the table.

"You want me to make you a plate?" Solis asked, nervous, unsure of how much she'd overheard.

"No. We had a potluck at work. I got a call from that Jackson woman. What's her name?"

"Ona, Dahlia. It's Ona."

"Yeah. She asked if you could babysit for them on the regular. Don't know why she called me."

"That's what moms do. They talk to other moms, get permission, check in—you know, parenting."

Irritation flashed across Dahlia's face. "You ain't a little kid. I said it was cool with me, but I can't be driving you way the hell out there every night."

"You won't have to. It'll just be on Fridays and this Saturday. They will pick me up and bring me back."

"How much are they paying you? You aren't quitting the candy shop, are you? We got bills. Cute little boys don't pay the rent."

"I'm not quitting. Marlon and I've worked it out. I always cover my expenses. Any other questions?"

Dahlia pushed her chair back from the table. "I'm going to bed. I'm working a double. See y'all tomorrow night. Make sure y'all clean this up."

Marlon waited until Dahlia closed her bedroom door. "Why don't you give her a break? You need to apologize for being a bitch just now."

"She can't pick and choose when she wants to be my mother. She was miffed the woman called her at all. No, cute little boys don't pay the rent, but they do pay for my clothes, my bus passes, and everything else I need so she doesn't have to."

"Apologize, Solis, I mean it."

"I will. Tomorrow."

"Your problem is you need to spend more time with people your own age. When does Iris get back from Arkansas?"

"Not sure, but before Cheer Camp. Why? Do you miss her, Marlon?" Solis asked, playfully.

"Iris has had a crush on me since you guys were in the first grade. She drives me crazy. But the two of you are good for each other. You get too old when she isn't around. And she gets too crazy without you."

"If you say so, Dad," Solis quipped, jokingly.

"Father does know best, you little brat. I cooked. You got dishes."

*****

Dahlia kicked off her shoes and fell into the recliner Solis and Marlon bought for her birthday. She didn't sleep well in beds; they gave her nightmares. Solis resisted anything and anyone she felt threatened her autonomy. She couldn't blame her. She'd raised Solis to depend on nothing and no one, not even her mother. A woman is safest when she is self-reliant. It was a lesson she'd learned the hard way.

Chapter 9

A summer sun set on the outdoor soirée. Guests mingled on the patio as servers in black and white weaved among them with beer and wine.

Distracted, Ronin leaned on the deck's railing. Solis and the boys were inside. He could see them through the French doors. He liked the way Solis' corset top and gypsy skirt gave a hint of the treasures beneath without spoiling the surprise. For a moment, he allowed himself to imagine Solis lying naked in his arms but quickly banished the picture from his mind. The feelings she stirred in him were so visceral, they made him uneasy.

"She's a rare beauty. Leave her alone." Byron handed Ronin a beer.

"What? Dad be serious. She's sixteen." Ronin sipped the beer to avoid looking his father in the eye. Byron could always tell when he was lying.

"That means nothing. In your mind, you've already crossed that line. You're a wolf, and quiet as its kept, some sheep go willingly to the slaughter."

"Said the fox to the wolf." Ronin smiled wryly. "There's nothing sheepish about Solis. If you met her, you'd know that."

"My days of raiding hen houses ended long ago."

"Not that long ago." Ronin laughed.

His father was an attractive man, tall and fit for his age. If it weren't for the salt and pepper of his hair, the two men would easily be indistinguishable. It was no secret between them that Byron had taken full advantage of it, often.

"Son, there are women who can possess a man. Drive him to commit acts of lunacy and foolishness. That little Lolita is one of them."

"Lolita?" Ronin scoffed. "You can tell all that just by looking at her, huh?"

"No. I can tell that by the way *you* look at her. I'm going to find your mother. You should go and find your wife." Byron walked away.

Ronin lingered awhile longer. His dad was right, and he knew it. He was long past foolishness and well on his way to lunacy.

*****

Ronin wasn't going to listen to him. He could see it in his eyes. That kind of desire had ruined many a man. Where in the world had this girl come from? How in the hell had she made a captive of his son? The questions begged for answers, and he had none to give. Byron made his way inside the house through the side door. He needed to meet this girl.

"Grandpa!" The boys jumped into Byron's arms.

"Goodness. Don't knock the old man over. Grandpa is happy to see you too."

Solis offered her hand. "You must be Grandpa. The boys have told me so much about you."

Byron returned the gesture. "Call me Byron."

"Solis Monroe. It's very nice to meet you. I was just about to get these boys off to bed. Boys, say good night to Grandpa."

"Good night, Grandpa." Robert gave Byron another hug. "Solis, can I pick the story tonight?"

"First one in the bed gets to pick," Solis replied.

Robert ran up the stairs as fast as his little legs could carry him. Ronin Jr. didn't.

"Bed? I'm not a baby." He pouted.

Byron whispered in his ear. "I understand. I'd rather spend time with a pretty girl too."

Ronin Jr. beamed and gave Byron another enthusiastic hug.

"Enough hugs. Off to bed with you. Don't give Solis any trouble."

"Okay." Ronin Jr. turned to Solis. "You know I'm going to beat him, right?"

"Yes, but be a good big brother and pick the book he wants . . . please?"

"Maybe," Ronin Jr. replied with a grin and hit the stairs.

Solis chuckled. "It was nice meeting you, Byron."

"You the same."

Byron headed for the bar in the den. Outside, the only offerings were beer and wine, and he had need of the stronger libations. He poured a whiskey neat and took a few sips.

A coinsure of women all his life, Byron knew innocence when he saw it. Solis lacked the confidence of a woman with her allure. But when her powers of seduction matured, she'd leave a trail of broken men in her wake, his son included.

Chapter 10

It was after ten when the last of the guests left for the evening. Solis wandered downstairs. She rounded the staircase, expecting to find Ronin waiting take her home. Instead, she found Ona and Joi, martinis in hand, laughing at the kitchen table. Solis cleared her throat to make her presence known.

"Ona, did you need any help before Mr. Jackson takes me home?"

"Who's this?" Joi snorted, clearly inebriated.

"Joi, I forgot to introduce you, this is Solis, our new sitter."

"Hello. Nice to meet you, Joi." Solis smiled.

"How old are you?" Joi asked, suddenly sober.

"Joi!" Ona exclaimed.

"I'm sixteen," Solis replied. "Ona, if you don't need anything—"

"No. No. It's late. Where's Ronin anyway?"

"Right here." Ronin stepped in as if on cue. "Come, let's get you home. I'll be back in a few." Ronin guided Solis out of the kitchen.

Joi turned to Ona. "Whose idea, was she? Please tell me not yours."

"Ours. Solis is wonderful with the boys. She comes on Friday nights so Ronin and I can go out. It's been great."

"I don't know, Ona. I wouldn't leave a temptation like that around my husband."

"Joi, she's sixteen. Ronin would never."

"I'm just saying. I'd find an older, less attractive babysitter. And I damn sure wouldn't let him drive her home . . . alone."

"Joi, I find, when a person begins or ends a statement with the words 'I'm just saying,' they probably shouldn't have said anything in the first place." Audra pulled out a chair.

After ten years of marriage, Ona had become accustomed to her mother-in-law's unsolicited pearls of wisdom and timely intrusions. Unfortunately, this time she walked in on Joi committing the cardinal sin—speaking ill of Ronin.

"Audra, Joi didn't mean it like that," Ona offered in a futile attempt to smooth things over.

"I see. Joi, where are the boys? I thought you might bring them to spend the night with their cousins." Audra's voice was cold and condescending.

"They're with their dad this weekend," Joi replied, her irritation obvious.

"And Marcus didn't join you? That's a shame. Please tell him I said hello. Ona, may I speak with you privately for a moment?" Audra asked, glaring at Joi.

"If you'll excuse me." Joi exited the table.

Anger seethed just below the surface of Ona's skin as she watched Joi leave the kitchen. She knew Audra wasn't overly fond of her, but through the years, their relationship had grown. But Joi? Joi was another story.

"Audra, she's my sister. I make no apologies for her. You'll respect my sister in my house," Ona snapped.

"You would do well to ensure Joi respects my son in his," Audra bit back.

"Mrs. Jackson, are you ready to retire for the evening?" Byron kissed Audra on the cheek.

Byron's sudden appearance cut short what was sure to be a heated conversation. Over the years, he'd gotten good at running interference between the two women. The key was never leave them alone together for too long.

"Yes. I am. Ona, it was a lovely party."

"Thank you." Ona kissed Audra on both cheeks. "Did you get to say good night to the boys?"

"No. I'll see them later. Kiss them for me. Good night. We'll see ourselves out."

"Yes. Good night, love." Byron hugged Ona.

"Will do. Good night."

Ona waved them out of the kitchen. Relieved, she called for Joi.

Joi stuck her head in the kitchen door. "Is the witch gone?"

"Yup. And not a moment too soon. Thank God for Byron."

"How on earth that man has stayed married to that woman all of these years is an enigma." Joi laughed.

Ona grabbed two wine glasses from the cabinet and an unfinished tray of hors d'oeuvres from the fridge. "The boys are asleep, the cleaning crew is coming in the morning, and Ronin won't be back for an hour. Feel like a sleepover?"

"Only if I get to put your bra in the freezer."

"You're an idiot." Ona laughed.

*****

Byron knew what was coming. Before he could start the car, Audra's damn burst.

"Joi is a crude and vulgar woman. She openly suggested that Ona get a new sitter because Ronin might be tempted by a sixteen-year-old girl! The nerve."

"Audra Lucille, calm down."

"Calm down? It was Joi's handiwork that sent Ona into your office that day. Or did you forget?"

"No, I haven't, but it's their marriage, Audra. Stay out of it."

Audra sat back in a huff. "Fine, but you will speak to Ronin about this. He needs to know that Joi is planting ideas in Ona's head again."

"I will, Audra, but you need to stay out of it. I'm his father. Let me handle it. Okay?"

"Okay."

Ordinarily, Audra's tantrums amused him but not tonight. However crude or vulgar, Joi was right. Solis needed to go—for her sake and for Ronin's.

Chapter 11

Ronin parked just around the corner from Solis' house.

"I missed you tonight. I wish you could've joined the party."

"Nope. The way you look at me, people would've noticed."

"Really?" Ronin asked, surprised. "I'm sorry if I made you uncomfortable."

"You didn't. I was fine, but your father . . . not so much. He came to see me. Fortunately, the boys ran interference."

"What? Sneaky SOB. I'm sorry."

"Don't be sorry. Just maybe don't look so much when other people are around."

"Point taken. I have something for you." Ronin handed her a thousand dollars.

"Whoa! What's this?"

"Two hundred dollars for the nanny, the going rate. The rest is to replace that dinosaur of a laptop with a notebook and to cover Cheer Camp."

"Ronin, I can't take this. It's too much."

"You can, and you will. If you don't, I'll just do it for you anyway."

"Okay, but if I take this, you can't pay me to babysit for a while. Got it?"

"Got it." Ronin grinned. He had no intention of doing that. If anything, he couldn't wait to find another reason to give her something. He was already thinking about her birthday.

"Cheer Camp starts in two weeks. I won't be free for our lunch dates on Saturdays. We'll have to pick another day."

"Not a problem. I'm not going to lie; I'd never have pegged you for a cheerleader."

"Why? Because I don't fit the stereotype? And here I thought you more enlightened. Most of my teammates don't. We're all smart girls."

"No. It isn't about the stereotype, it's more about personality, maturity. I don't see you having much in common with girls your age. I figure they'd get on your nerves after a while."

"Someone is paying attention." Solis laughed. "I do it because extracurricular activities are good on college applications. Believe it or not, they give scholarships for cheer. Cheerleading is an excellent way to stay fit and keep Marlon and Dahlia off my back about not being normal or having any normal friends. My best friend Iris and I have been doing it since junior high."

"Solis, you never cease to amaze me. Do you ever do anything 'just because'? No purpose, no thought behind it?"

"No. If that impresses you . . . wait until you see my pom-poms." Solis flashed him a devilish grin.

"You kill me, wicked girl."

"I should get going. Dahlia's home."

"I'll drive you to the door, but first . . ."

Ronin kissed her. Solis parted her lips, allowing him to caress her tongue with his. When she didn't hold back, he intensified the kiss, bringing her into the driver's seat with him. The taste and feel of her hardened him mercilessly. Without a word, he set Solis back in the passenger seat and drove around the corner.

"Ronin?"

He pressed a finger to her lips. "Solis, I need you to get out of the car and go inside. Do you understand?"

"I understand. Good night."

Ronin waited until Solis was safely inside and drove off. He pushed the speed limit, willing the car to move faster, faster than the overwhelming desire to turn around. Yet again, he'd have to exercise his lustful demons on an unsuspecting Ona. She enjoyed his exorcisms. Problem was, he didn't. The immediate need for release was satisfied, but the hunger, the desire for Solis remained. No amount of sex was going to change the fact that Ona wasn't Solis.

Chapter 12

"Will you never let go?" Dahlia forced the words through clinched teeth. It was a mistake opening the letter. Curiosity had gotten the better of her fear, and like the cat, it was killing her. Every word unlocked the nightmares she'd kept imprisoned deep within. She was there, screaming, tied to a bed, in the dark; waiting for the next monster to hurt her. She didn't know how long she'd been there when Darrell found her. He'd rescued her. He loved her. But had he? Did he? In the light of time and distance, she'd come to see things differently. If he hadn't made a whore and addict of her mother, how different might her life have been? Would she have needed his saving or loving at all? And there was Solis.

The day Solis was born, there was no joy, no happiness, no love. She was fourteen, and her world had ended. A nurse placed a sleeping pink bundle of a baby girl in her arms, and the pain of labor faded into a depthless sorrow. She'd thought about giving her up, but it felt cruel to abandon her. She decided then that if she couldn't love her, the least she could do was protect her. It was more than her mother ever did.

Hands shaking, Dahlia drank from the bottle, savoring the slow burn of the whiskey as it made its way down her throat. Bitterness and guilt from the inky blackness of a familiar sea broke on the shores of her heart. What kind of mother didn't love her own child?

*****

Solis checked the mail on the entry table as she came in the door. It was there, a letter from Iris. She'd finally written back. All it took was sending a self-addressed stamped envelope with her last letter. Iris, God love her, was lazy as hell.

Solis went to her room and set the letter and purse on the bed.

"Damn it." Solis cursed under her breath, realizing she'd left her favorite nighty in the dryer.

On her way to the laundry room, she heard what sounded like crying coming from Dahlia's room. Concerned, she rapped quietly on the door as she opened it. Dahlia was seated on the floor with some papers and a bottle of Jack Daniels in her hand.

"What are you doing up?" Solis asked, examining Dahlia's face closely. She rarely drank hard liquor. Something wasn't right. "What's wrong, Dahlia? What happened?"

"I got a letter from your father. He wants to talk to you."

"Is that it? Did you read it? Is he getting out?"

"Yes and no. I don't know why . . ."

Solis grabbed Dahlia, yanking her off the floor. "Come with me."

"Solis, where are we going?" Dahlia questioned; her words slurred. "You'll see."

In the kitchen, Solis turned a gas burner on high. "Burn it."

"What?"

"Burn it, Dahlia! Burn it! Burn it now!"

Solis forced Dahlia's hand over the flame; the paper lit, burning away quickly. Dahlia dropped it in the sink.

"What the hell, Solis?"

Before she could run water over it, Solis stopped her. "Watch it burn. Watch it, Dahlia."

Scared into submission, Dahlia watched the flames burn themselves out.

"What the hell is going on in here?" Marlon questioned them, rubbing the sleep from his eyes.

"Dahlia, I have no father. Darrell does not exist. Not for you. Not for me. I don't know everything he did, but I know what he did to you. You don't have to tell me. I've seen it on your face every day since I was old enough to understand. It didn't matter how good I was or what I did, nothing took that sadness from your eyes. Nothing. Do you think for one minute I'd ever let someone in my life who hurt you?"

Solis ran from the kitchen, angry tears falling. Marlon tried to stop her, but she shoved him away and ran to her room.

Dahlia turned on the faucet, adding her tears to the water as it circled the drain. She reached for the cabinet in search of an alcoholic salve for the wound Solis inflicted.

Marlon closed the cabinet. "No."

Dahlia fell to the floor, sobbing. Marlon joined her, cradling her in his arms.

He'd failed. He'd intercepted and destroyed every letter Darrell sent, but somehow, he'd missed this one. Ulayla must have given Darrell their address again.

The first letter broke Dahlia. He remembered the two days she'd spent lying in bed, almost catatonic. Solis would lie next to her, crying, begging Dahlia to eat, spoon-feeding her sips of water. The terror was still fresh in his mind. What if she died? What would happen to them? Would they end up back with Ulayla? Or worse, foster care? He swore he'd never let it happen again.

Dahlia's mental health was fragile. As children, he and Solis were often left to fend for themselves, when Dahlia's nightmares would leave her paralyzed for days at a time. She always managed to snap out of it, but it was hard on all of them, especially Solis.

It was quiet. Dahlia was asleep. Marlon carried her to her room and tucked her in bed, sure to leave the light on in case she woke up during the night. Dahlia was terrified of the dark.

He peeked in on Solis. She was asleep. Or at least that's what she wanted him to think. He closed her door and wandered back to the kitchen. This time he reached for the cabinet.

****

Solis opened her eyes once she was sure Marlon was gone. She was still angry, and the pain was raw. The last thing she needed was Marlon trying to guilt her into forgiving Dahlia. It wasn't that she didn't love Dahlia or understand her pain. But she'd discovered long ago that Dahlia was too broken to love her. She was a constant reminder of a terrible past Dahlia couldn't get over.

Solis checked her phone, desperately wanting to talk to Ronin; but it was too late. The letter from Iris lay beside her on the bed. She opened it.

Dear Solis,

> *Dear Solis, I swear that sounds corny. You got me writing letters like some* Little House on the Prairie *episode. I'll never get why you liked that damn show. Anyway, my grandmother's house is in the middle of nowhere. And when I say nowhere, I mean no cell service, dirt roads, and the nearest civilization is an hour away. Who doesn't have Wi-Fi, a movie theater, or a mall? I met a guy. A Trevor Jackson type with a Southern drawl and the charm to match. His name is Bobby. He's 18 and has his own car. I know what you're going to say, but we're having fun, and it's just a summer fling. I'll be back in two weeks before Cheer Camp. I can't wait. Miss you desperately. Write me again, it's lame, but I like it. I promise to write back.*

Miserable in Arkansas . . . Iris

Solis smiled; her spirits slightly lifted by the missive. "Eighteen? Try thirty-nine, married with kids."

Iris was into older guys, but she would die if she knew about Ronin. In truth, she probably wouldn't believe her. It didn't matter. She wasn't going to tell her. Ronin was her secret. Some secrets are too dangerous to share, even with your best friend.

Chapter 13

"Camp is killing me. Four hours a day, every other day is too much. I mean, why do I have to go? I don't even want to compete," Solis complained.

Iris sipped her smoothie. "This smoothie bar is heaven on earth. God, I missed California. Mangos, avocados, food that isn't fried or a fat bomb. We're outside in the middle of the day, and it isn't a sauna. The left coast is the best coast."

"Did you hear a word I said?" Solis asked, perturbed.

"Quit your bitchin'. You're one of the best. If you don't compete, we won't win."

"Bitchin'? I only do this cheer stuff to keep you and Dahlia happy. And you haven't done anything but complain about Arkansas for the last two days. Like it's some third-world country."

"Oh, sis, where my Nana lives, it is."

"I don't want to hear it. You had a tall, dark, and handsome distraction."

"It'll never be the same. Older is so much better." Iris did a lizard lick with her tongue.

"Stop! Who are you, and what have you done with my Iris?"

"Don't be such a virgin. You need a man. If you were on more social media, you'd get out more . . . meet more people . . . have a clue. Did you do anything fun this summer while I was gone?"

"I don't want or need to share my every thought, meal, activity, or whatever with the world. Something you narcissistic, selfie-obsessed exhibitionist can't understand. Most guys only want one thing anyway. I'm not giving it away to some stupid high school boy. And fun is relative."

"You and your five-dollar words. Solis, you're so odd. It's a good thing you're hot."

"Are you seriously suggesting that no guy would want me if I was just smart? Misogynism much? You aren't an ugly duckling. Your Coke-bottle shape and pretty eyes keep the boys calling."

"Yeah, but not like you. Boys dream about you . . . they stutter, act dumb, and stare when the see you. I'm not jealous, but it's not the same, and you know it."

"Iris, it isn't the same. Boys focus on your appearance and never bother to get to know the you inside."

"That's because they're boys. Now you see why I like older guys. They've got more on their minds than sex. Speaking of boys, look who's coming . . . Rondé and Trey."

"What have we here? Y'all is all kind of fine. How's a brotha supposed to stay in the game with all this on the sideline?" Rondé asked.

"Rondé." Solis rolled her eyes.

"Come on, Solis, don't be like that. Come to the movies tonight with me and Trey."

"Yeah, show a little school spirit." Trey laughed, giving Rondé a fist bump.

Iris shot Solis a wicked look. "We'll go. What movie? What time?"

"Whatever's playing." Trey smiled triumphantly.

"Cool. We'll meet you there around seven. Now go away." Iris giggled.

Trey and Rondé shuffled off, chest puffed out like two cocky roosters.

"Iris! Are you nuts? I'm not going. Rondé is a ho. And Trey? Trey is slow. What happened to older is better?"

"They're tall, cute, and on the basketball team. We're cheerleaders, we're supposed to date guys like them. It's just a movie. I'll come over, and we'll get ready together. We'll swing by my house and grab a few things. God knows what's in your closet. Do you even own a makeup bag? After the movie, I'll spend the night, we can go shopping downtown tomorrow."

"Fine, but I have to work tomorrow at seven."

"Tell that fine-ass cousin of yours to let you off. It's one day."

"No. I got another job, working as a nanny for a family in The Willows. Remember?"

"Damn, Solis, don't you work enough?"

"If I was a spoiled little daddy's girl like you, I wouldn't have to."

"Don't hate. Besides, at least Dahlia leaves you alone. Mine are all over me. Well, since you have two jobs, you should have plenty of money to spend on real clothes."

"Iris, a girl's got expenses, and then there's college."

"Stop adulting already. We're going to the movies and shopping. No adulting this weekend. Let's go."

Solis tossed her smoothie in the trash. Adulting—that summed up her entire life. She'd been adulting for as long as she could remember. Iris didn't get it. Freedom wasn't free.

"Solis, I know you don't think I get it."

"I didn't say that."

"You didn't have to. How long have we been friends? Your life is harder than mine, I could never deal with what you do. But I refuse to let you mope around and feel sorry for yourself."

"I love you, Iris."

"Of course, you do. I'm awesome."

Chapter 14

Marlon rummaged through the clothes on Solis's bed. "I wish you'd let me dress you, like when you were little. Your wardrobe is . . . sad."

"Here we go. You and Iris. I swear. My clothes aren't sad . . . they're inexpensive."

"I've seen your paycheck; you can afford better."

"Check the bags on the nightstand. Iris and I picked out a few new things. I hate shopping with her. She's always trying to make me naked."

"Solis, you need to stop trying to hide your body from the world. Dahlia too, always walking around in those scrubs. Bitches pay money to look like the two of you do naturally and don't even come close."

"I don't like the attention. Men always get the wrong idea."

"You still get attention. You got Ronin's attention. And you were wearing your uniform."

"Shut up, Marlon. Here." Solis tossed a manicure set at him. "Make yourself useful."

"I get to pick the color." Marlon sorted the small bottles of polish.

"No color. It always chips. French."

"It only chips because you wear it too long."

"Whatever, just paint them, okay? I need them dry before Ronin gets here. I'm babysitting tonight."

"That brother got it bad for you, girl."

"He likes me. I don't know about having it bad. He's a married man. He loves his wife and his children."

"One thing has nothing to do with the other."

49

"Marlon, the whole world isn't a soap opera."

"Older man cheating on his wife with his underage nanny? That's a Lifetime movie in the making."

"You got me there."

"You're falling for him. I can see it."

"I just like being with him. He's sweet. So why aren't you telling me to stay away from him or that he is married and too old for me?"

"I thought about it. Solis, no boy your age is ever going to make you happy. You're too old for them. Hell, sometimes you're too old for me. I know you. Crazy as it sounds, being a kept woman suits you. You have your head on straight. You're happy. He isn't hurting you. So why trip?"

"What about his wife?"

"What about her? She was on her way out long before you."

"I should feel bad. I really like her. It's strange."

"Why should you? You aren't married to her. He is. You aren't trying to take him away from her. He's leaving on his own."

Solis kissed his cheek. "I love you, Marlon."

"Right back at you. Oh, but on big brother thing . . . pill?"

"Every day."

"Good girl. Getting your swerve on is one thing . . . Babies are something else."

Chapter 15

Solis walked down the stairs to the street where Ronin was waiting. Relaxed on the door of his Jaguar, in khaki chinos and a sage untucked shirt, Ronin was every bit *GQ*. Solis could feel his gaze, warm and intense. It gave her butterflies when he eyed her that way. She wanted to run into his arms but knew better. They weren't alone.

"Hey, beautiful." Ronin smiled as she approached.

"Hey yourself. What are you and Ona up to tonight?"

"Nothing."

"Nothing?"

"Tonight, I'm taking you on a proper date."

"Ona? The boys?"

"Ona is out of town, and the boys are where all grandchildren should be—with their grandparents."

"Wow. It is just you and me?"

"Yup. Feel like dinner and a movie?"

"Of course. Where to?"

"T'italiano I hear it is the best place to get authentic Italian." Ronin opened her door. "Get in. I have a surprise for you."

"Don't you spoil me enough?"

"Solis Monroe, I haven't even begun to spoil you."

****

Dinner at l'italiano was worth the forty-five-minute drive to Lofland. The dark wood and stone interior gave the restaurant a quaint old world feel. They sat at a small candle lit table for two. The food was amazing. To both their surprise the waiter didn't even blink when Solis ordered the complimenting Chablis to her shrimp linguine. It was perfect.

The surprise was a drive-in theater. Like Lofland it was a little out of the way, but blankets on a grassy knoll was far more romantic than a dark theater and buttered popcorn.

Solis curled up in Ronin's arms under the blanket. The scent of vanilla and jasmine on her hair and skin was intoxicating. Ronin couldn't resist. He moved the braid from her neck and gently kissed her collarbone. Solis turned her head, offering her neck and shoulder to him. Emboldened by her reaction, Ronin turned Solis in his arms, taking her lips with his. Her skin in full fever, she hungrily returned his kisses.

Stop! Stop now! the voice in his head screamed. Ronin released her. Solis repined in subtle protest, stiffening his painful erection.

"Ronin?" Solis whispered the question, her eyes a mixture of confusion and desire.

"Why? Because I brought you here to watch a movie? If it ever comes to that, it won't be at a drive-in."

"Ronin, I didn't mean to—"

"I wasn't playing fair."

"No, you weren't." Solis smiled.

"It's late. When is Dahlia expecting you home?"

"Not until after eleven. It doesn't matter anyway; she won't be home until six or so tomorrow morning. We can finish the movie, if you still want to."

"Of course, I do. Come here." Ronin wrapped his arms and the blanket around her. "I promise I'll keep my hands to myself."

Solis was a passionate woman. She was too inexperienced to know it, but he wasn't. Taking her to bed would ruin him. There would be no woman after her.

Chapter 16

Solis stepped off the 85 line at Denton Park and 53rd and walked the block to George Washington Preparatory on 54th. Ona offered to send a car service; but Solis declined, opting to take the bus instead. The last thing she wanted was to draw attention to herself. Getting picked up from school by a chauffeur would feed the rumor mill, and she had no intention of becoming one of its victims.

Solis waited by the school gate for Ronin Jr. and Robert to be dismissed.

An older portly man in a black suit and tie approached Solis from a black on chrome Chrysler 300 with limo-dark windows.

"Ms. Monroe? My name is Christopher, I'm your driver."

"You'll understand if I insist on seeing your identification?" Solis replied.

Christopher handed Solis his license. "Not at all. I was a bit thinner back then." He smiled, patting his belly.

Solis examined his ID. The round chocolate teddy bear with cherub cheeks and salt and pepper fur in front of her still resembled the slimmer man in the photo.

"Thank you." Solis gave the license back to him.

"No problem. I'll take your bag and wait for you and the boys by the far gate." Christopher tipped his hat and left.

"Solis!" Robert jumped down the stairs and ran through the gate, straight into Solis's arms.

"If it isn't my favorite little Lost Boy. I'm happy to see you too." Solis searched the sea of red and khaki uniforms. "Where is Ronin?"

"Here I am!" Ronin Jr. waved. "Sorry I'm late. Had to get a book from the library."

"Now that we're all here, let's go. Christopher is just down around the corner."

Robert took Solis' hand. "I wish you went to school with us. There are high school kids at our school too."

"That'd be nice, but I like my school. All my friends are there."

GWP, as the locals called it, was Denton's exclusive private school. Few got in to GWP, but Solis had. In eighth grade, she sat for the exams and interview, but even with scholarships, they couldn't afford the tuition. It was disappointing but gave her a burning determination that when it came to college, she wouldn't miss out on the opportunity.

*****

Robert spent the whole ride home telling Solis about his day and all the exciting things GWP had. Ronin Jr. sat in quiet disinterest until Solis asked him about the book he checked out of the library. A bookworm, he loved to read. Solis, having read all the books before, gave him someone to talk to. Once home, they settled around the kitchen table for snacks and homework.

"Solis, I don't get this. Mrs. Adamson wants me to tell her what I want to be when I grow up. I don't know what I want to be when I grow up. I'm not grown-up yet," Robert puzzled.

"When I was your age, they used to ask me the same question. I thought it was dumb. I mean, the only thing I wanted to be when I grew up was me. Don't tell your teacher I said that. What they're really asking is, 'What do you want to do when you grow up?'"

"A lawyer. I want to be a lawyer," Ronin Jr. answered.

"Yeah, a lawyer," Robert added.

Solis shook her head. It was clear their answers were well rehearsed. "Why do you want to be a lawyer?"

"Because our dad and grandpa are lawyers. We have to be lawyers too," Ronin Jr. answered.

"No, you don't. You can do whatever you want to do. If you could do anything, anything at all, what would it be?"

"I want to make things that people like to eat."

"A chef—that's an excellent idea. You should write that down. Ronin Jr., what about you?"

Ronin Jr. didn't answer right away. It was obvious the idea of doing whatever he wanted to do when he grew up was new to him.

"Something to do with books," he offered, unsure of himself.

"You could be a writer, a publisher, a teacher. I think you would make a great teacher."

"Teacher?"

"Absolutely. You teach me something new every time we read together. You two finish your homework. When you're done, you can watch TV. I'll clean up from snack and work on my own homework."

"You have homework too?" Robert asked, shocked.

"Yes. I have homework. Homework never goes away."

Robert put his head down. "That's depressing."

Solis laughed. "Yes, yes, it is."

****

Ona was late. Solis tried reaching her by phone several times with no luck. She was getting nervous. Tonight's football game was the biggest of the season—George Washington Prep versus Roosevelt High. GWP beat Roosevelt at everything, except sports. For all of George Washington's recruitment efforts, lavish gym, and stadium, Roosevelt always came out on top athletically. It was a source of great pride for the school.

"It's six o' clock, Solis. Where the hell are you? The game starts at seven," Iris asked, annoyed.

"I know. I know. What do you want me to do? Mrs. Jackson isn't here yet."

"Call, Mr. Jackson then. Tell one of them to come get their kids, or I'm coming to get you, and the kids will have to come with us."

"Calm down. I'll call again. I'll call you when I'm on the way."

Iris was irritated. Solis was too. If she'd known Ona was going to be late, she'd never have agreed to get the boys. She'd brought her cheer uniform and everything else she needed with her, but if Ona didn't show up soon, she'd be late. Solis was calling Ona again when Ronin came in.

"Great! You're here. Ona isn't here yet, and I have a football game tonight. Will you give me a ride to school? The game starts in an hour. I thought Ona would be home by now."

"What are you doing here?"

"Ona text me this afternoon and asked if I'd get the boys. She had some big meeting she couldn't miss. Christopher brought us home. Ronin, I really need to go."

"Sorry. Yes. I'll take you. As a matter of fact, we'll all go. Boys, how'd you like to go to a real football game?"

Ronin Jr. jumped off the couch. "Yes! I want to go but only on one condition."

Ronin was surprised. It was unusual for Ronin Jr. to be that excited about anything. "And what's that, Chief?"

"As long as I get to eat anything I want," he stated flatly.

"Me too," Robert added.

Ona had everyone in the house on a strict diet. Football game concessions were not on the menu.

"Deal. Let's go." Ronin shooed them up the stairs. "Get your coats."

"You may want to grab a few heavy blankets. It gets cold quick." Solis grabbed the rest of her things.

"I will. What about you? However sexy, that skirt can't possibly keep you warm. Don't you have sweats or a track suit or something?"

"I go to Roosevelt, not GWP. We're going to win, so I'll have a lot to cheer about. The constant movement will help a bit."

"Dad! Let's go!" Ronin Jr. grabbed Ronin's hand, dragging him toward the door.

"Okay, Chief. Okay. Everyone in the car."

****

Ona set her things down. She felt bad. Things went off the rails at work, and she'd forgotten all about the boys and Solis. Solis called and text numerous times, but she hadn't noticed her phone was off. Fortunately, Ronin made it home in time to get Solis to her game.

"Where is everybody?"

Ona wandered through the living room into the kitchen. The boys' schoolwork was stacked neatly on the kitchen table, clean dishes from dinner sat in the dish drain. But there was no sign of anyone. The house was quiet.

Ona glanced at her phone. Solis hadn't text and there was nothing from Ronin either. She called Ronin, no answer. She text him, no reply. She tried Solis, nothing. "What the hell?" Ona tried calling again, but it went straight to voice mail.

Ona was starting to worry when the garage door alarm sounded. Ona checked the clock. "You got to be kidding me?"

Ronin walked in carrying a sleeping Robert, with Ronin Jr. behind him talking a mile a minute.

"Mom! Mom! It was so awesome. There were these big lights on the field so you could see everything. People were cheering. Solis' school won. She introduced us to all her cheerleader friends. She even let Robert use one of her pom-poms. There was a stand with hot chocolate, candy, hot dogs, and nachos. Robert didn't finish his hot dog. He fell asleep like a big baby. I ate the rest of it and shared Dad's nachos. Can we go again? Please."

"Okay, Chief. We can tell Mommy more about it tomorrow. Time for bed. Ona, I'll be right back. Got to put this one down."

Ona couldn't believe it. Ronin kept the boys out past their bedtime, let them sit out in the cold, eat junk, and play with cheerleaders. By the time Ronin made it back downstairs, she was seething.

"Wow, baby. We had a good time. I didn't think the boys would enjoy it that much. It was dark and cold, but they had a great time,

Ronin Jr. especially. I'm sorry I didn't take them to a game sooner. I had no idea they could eat so much. We must not be feeding them enough."

"Tomorrow, when they're tired, have tummy aches and colds, are you going to stay home to take care of them?" Ona snapped.

"One night out a football game won't hurt them." Ronin replied.

"You should've told me. And you know how I feel about junk food."

"When do I need your permission to take my sons anywhere? Or let them eat anything?"

"I didn't mean for it to come out the way it sounded."

"Yes, you did. You want to go there? Since when did Solis start picking the boys up from school, doing homework, and making dinner? Isn't that your job? I do the morning routine; you do the afternoon."

"I had a meeting . . . time got away from me."

"Three hours? Why didn't you call me? Or at least Solis. She was doing you a favor."

"Would you have answered if I had? You didn't even text me to tell me where you were."

"If it was about the boys and getting Solis to school, yes." Ronin grabbed his keys and headed for the garage. "Where are you going?" Ona asked, frantic.

"None of your buisness."

"Don't talk to me like that. What the hell is wrong with you? Where—"

"Where? The hell away from you before I say something . . . you can't control everything, Ona." Ronin slammed the door.

The last thing Ona heard was the sound of his car driving off at a high rate of speed. Alone, standing in the foyer, an overwhelming sense of panic engulfed her. He'd never left before.

Chapter 17

Walking around in the dark for hours, knocking on strangers' doors, was not Ona's idea of a good time. When Solis suggested they bring the boys to the mall for Halloween, she thought it was a brilliant idea, but fifteen stores in, she was over it.

"I never realized how many stores were in this mall."

"Ona, why don't you go to the café and relax? I can take the boys around," Ronin offered.

"No, let's get through this line. I'm anxious to see what surprise Solis has for the boys."

The boys adored Solis. They'd be devastated if she didn't come and see their Tinker Bell. And after the football debacle, she knew Ronin would be upset too.

It didn't take long to reach the front of the line. Once there, it was clear why the line for the candy store was so long. Solis stood at the entrance in a green pixie dress, complete with wings, slippers, and a wand that dropped gold and silver confetti as pixie dust. Face paint reminiscent of Mardi Gras sparkled around her eyes, and her lips shimmered a blush rose. Marlon stood next to her in full pirate regalia. He was Captain Hook from the wig on his head down to the high heeled boots on his feet. Together, they stayed in character and interacted with every child who came to the store front. Everyone was thrilled, kids and parents alike.

"Peter Pan, I have been waiting for you! You brought a Lost Boy with you, splendid. Captain Hook has been a lot for a little pixie like me to handle."

"Argh! Don't be listening to her. She is a meddlesome pixie," Marlon growled.

"Would you boys and girls like some chocolate gold?"

"Yes!" the children cried in unison.

"Smead! Smead! She's giving away me gold!" Marlon cried, pretending to look for his henchmen Smead.

Bobby hurried from the back of the store, a disheveled Smead, with Piper, a proper Wendy on his heels.

"The only way pixies can give away pirate gold is if you say the magic words," Solis prompted the children.

A chorus of "Trick or Treat!" filled the shop.

Marlon, Bobby, Piper, and Solis gave out handfuls of chocolate gold coins to every excited child.

Ona gazed on the store front in amazement. "Solis, this is absolutely wonderful!"

"How on earth did you make the store front into a real pirate ship?" Ronin asked.

"That was the hard part. Getting Marlon to wear heels was easy."

"Who you kidding? Walking in these boots isn't easy. Solis don't be too long. We got a lot of customers." Marlon resumed his Captain Hook persona and went back into the store.

"I'm so glad you came to see me. You two make the best Lost Boy and Peter Pan I've ever seen." Solis knelt and hugged them both.

"Can we take your picture? Please?" Ronin Jr. asked.

"Sure, but only if you're in it."

The boys stood next to Solis. She sat on her knees to make sure they were all in the picture.

"Say cheese." Ronin snapped the photo.

"Well, Peter and my little Lost Boy, Captain Hook needs my help. I'll see you guys next week. Don't eat too much candy. My pixie wand doesn't work on tummy aches or cavities." Solis kissed each of them on the forehead. "Thanks for bringing them. See you guys later."

Ona touched Ronin on the shoulder. "She is nothing short of amazing."

"She is something special," Ronin replied.

"I'll go to the café. Go ahead and take the boys around some more."

"Come on, Daddy, let's go!" Robert begged, pulling at Ronin's sleeve.

"Are you sure?" Ronin asked, puzzled by Ona's sudden change of mood.

"Go."

"Dad, Solis is awesome! Can we go back?" Ronin Jr. beamed.

"I'm glad you think so. Maybe on our way out to say goodbye. Let's go, Chief. Ona, we won't be too long, promise."

*****

Ona ordered a peppermint mocha and took a seat. The café wasn't full, but it was obvious a lot of other parents had the same idea.

"Join me." A woman at the next table motioned for Ona to come over. She debated for a moment and decided to move. "I'm Myriam. You waiting for a husband and kids too?"

"I'm Ona. Yeah, I tapped out after the candy store."

"OMG, they really knocked it out of the park this year. My daughter Melissa loved it. She made my husband take her back to see Tinker Bell twice! The mall should really put them in charge of the whole thing."

"My boys too. Tinker Bell is our sitter. She's great. She even made the boys' costumes."

"She's your sitter? Does she sit for other families?"

"No. Just ours. Solis has a lot on her plate with high school and her part-time job at the store."

"High school? I can guarantee the boys in her classes aren't learning anything." Myriam laughed.

"Probably not. I know she's made our lives easier. The boys love her."

"Honey, you ready to go?" Myriam's husband approached.

"Ona, this is my husband Edward. Back so soon?"

"Yeah, things got a little testy at the candy store. Some trick-or-treaters tried to get a little too friendly with Tinker Bell and Wendy, Captain Hook and some dad in line handled it. Speak of the devil. Hey, my good man." Edward offered his hand to Ronin as walked up.

"Hey. Good to meet you. Ona, let's go."

"Myriam, Edward, this is my very irritated husband, Ronin. What happened? Is Solis okay?"

"Grown men acting a fool! One of them grabbed her! Grabbed her! And wouldn't let go! I couldn't . . . I need to leave. It was nice meeting both of you."

"Okay. It's been lovely, Myriam."

Edward waited until Ronin and Ona were out of earshot. "Is Tinker Bell his daughter?"

"No. Ona says she's their babysitter."

"Maybe, but she's also his mistress."

"Edward! Don't say that. You don't know that."

"Myriam, a man doesn't react the way he did unless the woman is his wife or his daughter. Since she's neither, the only thing left is mistress."

"She's in high school, Edward."

"That poor bastard is going to jail."

Chapter 18

Seven months in and Saturday lunches in the mall were now lazy afternoons. When Ona was out of town, they'd go out or, like today, hang around the house.

"Where are you going for Thanksgiving?" Ronin asked.

"Ulayla will insist we come to her house. Marlon and I will go. Dahlia will go to work for the overtime. She would walk in traffic to avoid walking on the same side of the street as Ulayla."

"From what you've told me, I don't blame her. Why do you go?"

"Obligation. She's our grandmother. Awful as she is, without her, who knows how we would've ended up? Choking down her dry turkey and mushy stuffing once a year is a small sacrifice. She does make a killer sweet potato pie."

"Remind me never to complain about my in-laws ever again."

"You guys going to Byron and Audra's house?"

"Yes. I wish you could go with us."

"Nope. Me, you, and Ona together? Terrible idea."

"You are wise beyond your years."

Ronin rolled Solis on top of him and kissed her. The way her body responded to his forced him to pull away. He could see the letdown on her face.

"Solis, we can't. We just can't."

"Is it because I'm sixteen? Or because I'm a virgin?"

Ronin cupped Solis's face with his hands. "I love you, and one day, when the time is right, we will make love. Now is not that time."

"Damien will be here soon. You should take me home."

Solis was frustrated. He knew it. But unlike him, she didn't have an Ona to go home to. It was unfair. He needed to give her the release, she hadn't yet learned to give herself.

"Solis." Ronin slid off the couch on to his knees and held out his hand. "Sit on your knees with your back to me."

Ronin drew her to him, securing her waist with one hand and separating her legs with the other. Solis froze.

"Do you want me to stop?" he asked quietly.

Solis shook her head.

Ronin slipped his hand under the top of her yoga pants and panty. Solis grabbed his hand.

He smiled. "Let go."

She did. He searched her with his hand, massaging her clitoris softly at first, slowly increasing and decreasing; the speed and pressure. Solis rode his palm in rhythm with his touch. Rolling her hair around his hand, he turned her to face toward him. The fire in her chocolate eyes told him all he needed to know. Solis was his.

Solis convulsed in his arms; he forced his tongue as deep in her mouth as it would go, drinking in her cry. Solis pushed back with surprising force. Ronin gave way, letting her push him on to his back. She ran her hands over his swollen cock.

"Show me, please," Solis pleaded.

He could have her now; teach her to taste him, sheathe himself inside her until they were one, revel in the heat of her skin on his tongue and the sound of her pleasure in his ears. He was spiraling.

The gate bell rang. Damien was early.

Ronin gently pulled Solis away. "I love you."

"I love you too. What are we going to do about Damien?"

"I'll figure something out. Go."

Solis collected her clothing and rushed off to clean up.

Ronin took a minute to compose himself before making his way to the kitchen. He stepped to the sink, tapped the faucet, and let it run hot. He smothered his hands in dish soap and plunged them beneath the scalding water. The burn settled his mind and body.

Damien saved him. He was grateful, but he wasn't happy. Now he needed to figure out how to explain Solis. Damien wouldn't care that he was stepping out on Ona, but he would care that Solis was underage. *You knew this was going to happen.*

Damien let himself in and wandered into the kitchen.

"Ro, when you called, I was shocked. You with the whole house to yourself. I don't believe it."

"You're early."

"That's a problem?"

Solis peeked her head around the kitchen door, smiling. "Hello, Damien."

"Oh shit!" Startled, Damien stumbled back.

"Do you always greet people like that?" Solis chided him.

"No. But in my defense, beautiful women don't usually appear in my brother's kitchen out of thin air."

"You're sweet. My name is Solis. It's nice to meet you. Ronin, I'm ready to go."

Ronin picked up his keys. "Damien, I'll be back in thirty."

"I'll be here. It was nice meeting you, Solis."

"You too."

* * *

Solis was quiet, not a natural state for her. Worried, Ronin stopped the car. "Are you okay?"

"No. What are you going to tell him?"

"As little as possible."

"You're going to need to tell him more than that."

Solis was right. He knew the jig was up the moment he saw his brother's face. Damien was like a dog with a bone when he wanted to know something. There would be no avoiding the conversation.

"Don't worry about Damien. He's my brother. I'll handle it."

"He knows. I could see it in his eyes. He's going to make you leave me."

Ronin touched Solis' cheek. "Never going to happen. It'll be fine. Trust me."

Solis closed her eyes. "I'm sorry."

"For what?"

"I teased you. I acted like a—"

"No. No. No. Baby, no. You did nothing wrong. If anything, I was wrong. I told you we couldn't, and then I touched you."

"I wanted you to."

"I know you did. I did too."

"It's going to be a long year." Solis smiled.

"Yes, but you . . . you are worth the wait." Ronin smiled back.

"I love you, Ronin."

"I love you too."

Chapter 19

"Are we going to talk about this?" Damien asked, handing Ronin a beer.

"There's nothing to talk about."

"Yeah, right. She's perfection. A little young, didn't figure you for the coed type, but a man would be a fool to let that get away. Where did you meet her?"

"None of your business."

"Come on. You got to tell me."

"Solis is . . . I just want to keep her to myself for now."

"It's like that? How long has this been going on?"

"Goddamn, you just won't let up. Since May."

"And you're just telling me this now?"

"If you weren't early, you still wouldn't know."

"Why all the secrecy? What aren't you telling me? Or more importantly, why aren't you telling me? I'm your brother, Ro, you know you can trust me."

"I know. This . . . this is different. Solis is . . . just let it go, Damien. Please."

"Different? Men cheat on their wives all the time. I know I would. What could be so different that you couldn't tell . . .?" The truth fell on Damien like lead weight. "Tell me she's legal."

"She's legal."

"Don't lie to me!" Damien shouted angrily. "How old is she?"

"Don't ask questions you already know the answers to, counselor."

Damien rushed Ronin, knocking him to the floor. The two struggled until Ronin gained the upper hand. Pinned face-first to the hardwood, Damien tapped out.

"You still hit like a bitch?"

Ronin helped him up. "You still wrestle like one? Another beer?"

Damien rolled his eyes. "I need something harder than that for this shit."

"Me too. Come with me."

In the den, Ronin poured them both a shot of whisky. He drowned his quickly, poured another, and did the same. He filled the tumbler again, slowly this time, giving the liquid courage time to build.

"Sixteen. She'll be seventeen next month"

"Are you trying to go to jail? Are you crazy?" Damien shouted incredulously.

"I know what you're thinking. I'm in love with her."

"In love? Ro, she's sixteen. What could you possibly have in common with this girl?"

"It isn't about what we have in common. I can't explain it. I need her. The boys love her. Ona does too."

"You brought my nephews into this shit?"

"I convinced Ona to hire her as our sitter. Keep your wife close and your mistress closer . . . Is that how it goes?"

"Oh, this just gets better and better. And Ona isn't suspicious? Of course, she isn't. If she was, you'd be in jail or dead. You've been sleeping with this girl for seven months? Is that what I interrupted?"

"Yes, you interrupted. But it's a good thing. If you hadn't . . . I was slipping, it takes all I have not to. The idea of being the first does shit to me."

"She's a virgin? You took her right out of the damn cradle! Man, I got a black book full of women who know how to keep it on the low. Grown women. Where are her parents?"

"Her family situation is complicated. It's hard to explain."

"Don't tell me single mom, dad not in the picture?"

Ronin poured Damien another drink. "How'd you know that?"

"No father would let a girl like that hang out in the middle of the day without supervision. She'd be a prime target for every Tom, Dick, and Ronin out there."

"You're right about her home life. No mother-of-the-year awards there. She does have an older cousin; he looks after her."

"Does he? If she's with you, he can't be doing too good a job. And as for her mother, you aren't winning any father-of-the-year awards either. I mean, keep it real . . . The boys' underage babysitter? I'm a criminal defense attorney, an officer of the court. If you weren't my brother, I'd turn you in. You know how many men I've represented that got caught up? I never, in a million years, thought I'd have to add you to the list. Ro, this girl could ruin your whole life. You swear you aren't sleeping with her? Swear it?"

"I swear it. I'll wait. I have to."

"Wait? Not with that . . . no man could, especially you. You could really hurt this girl."

"You don't know, Solis. I'd never hurt her. Ever. Solis is as bright as she is beautiful. Wise beyond her years."

"She isn't a woman. However intelligent and mature she may be, it doesn't change the fact that she's a girl. You're taking advantage of her naivety. You're an asshole. Fire her. In a year, if you still want it, call her For now, get as far away from her as you can. For her sake and yours."

"I can't."

"Can't or won't?"

"Both."

"If you don't, I'll—"

"Careful, brother. Solis is mine. I'll lay waste to anyone who tries to take her from me, including you."

"Are you serious? This is going to end badly. You know that, right? Think about it."

"Maybe. Probably. You don't understand. Solis is—"

"Sixteen. She is sixteen, Ronin."

"I know."

Damien sat silent. Ronin was infatuated with Solis. It wasn't about the sex. It wouldn't matter if he dropped his brother in a harem full of beautiful women willing and able to fulfill his every desire; Ronin would claw his way out and find Solis. And once he had her, it was over. A sixteen-year-old girl held his brother's life in her hands. He had to talk Ronin out of this madness. If he couldn't, his big brother would soon be one of his clients.

Chapter 20

"You're home early. Everything okay?" Solis closed the door. Dahlia never came home early. Sick or tired, she worked. It was strange.

"Overtime was cancelled. Marlon just left. Where've you been?"

"At the Jacksons'."

"You've been over there a lot. You saving that money? We got—"

"Bills. I know. I put money in the house account last month. I'll put in another two hundred when I get paid. Dahlia, we have the same conversation every time we talk. Iris is coming over in about an hour to do homework. After that, let's go out—my treat."

Solis hoped Dahlia would take her up on the offer. They hadn't had a real conversation since the letter-burning incident. Today she'd make the effort, if for no other reason than to keep Dahlia off her case.

"Your treat?"

"My treat. Anywhere you want. Think of it as a girls' night." Solis smiled. "If overtime is cancelled, you don't have anything to do."

"I guess so. I'll take a nap. Wake me up when you guys are ready to go."

"Hell no! You go in there and turn that Pinto you pretend to be, back into the Ferrari that you are. You might meet Mr. Right."

"Solis, you're nuts. The last thing I need is a man."

"Dahlia, the first thing you need is man. Now go. I'll settle for a Mercedes."

"How 'bout a Corolla?" Dahlia laughed.

"Nope. Do you want me to sic Iris on you?"

Dahlia put her hands up. "Please, God, not Iris. I'll figure something out."

"Good. Now go."

Dahlia left for her room. Solis did the same. It'd been a long time since she'd heard Dahlia laugh. It felt good.

Solis stripped down. She needed to shower. Iris would be over shortly, and Ronin's scent, like his touch, lingered on her skin.

"He's my brother. I'll handle it." Ronin's words echoed in Solis' head. Damien was a problem, even if Ronin didn't want to admit it. She checked her phone, curious to know how things went. No messages. She started to text him but thought better of it. If he hadn't text her, that meant the inquisition wasn't over. She'd have to wait.

****

Still smiling, Dahlia took a seat at the antique dressing table Solis bought for her. Solis loved old things. Her room was an eclectic mix of old books and antique furniture she'd found at garage sales and flea markets. If she'd let her, Solis would turn the whole house into an antique shop.

Dahlia brushed the dust from the mirror. She turned away, her smile fading. It was Marie. She could see her mother in her eyes, and it hurt.

Dahlia could feel the clouds forming, threatening to take her to that dark place. They always did when she spent too much time thinking. She was moments from surrendering when Solis popped her head in the door.

"Not tonight, Dahlia. You're going to enjoy yourself. Get it together, or I swear I'll send Iris in there with a makeup bag and a mission." Solis closed the door.

"Okay. Okay. I got it. I promise," Dahlia called after her.

Dahlia wasn't surprised by Solis sudden appearance at the door. From a young age, Solis was keenly aware of Dahlia's mood swings, often sensing them before they happened. She'd never say it, but there were times that Solis was all that stood between her and death by her own hand.

Dahlia faced the mirror. "Pinto my ass."

Chapter 21

Ona lay in bed, her long, slender frame coiled around Ronin. An amazing lover, Ronin could pleasure a woman into delirium. Intuitive, he knew what a woman wanted before she did. A master of the female form, he knew just where to touch and where to taste. After ten years, nothing had changed. If anything, the sex was better, especially of late.

"Remember when you'd sneak into my dorm? We'd make love just like this."

"I remember falling off an ivy-covered trellis trying to avoid your resident assistant."

"That was hilarious!"

"To you. My back hurt for a week."

"It seems so long ago."

"Twelve years is a long time." Ronin breathed deeply.

"I've got an idea. Come with me to San Diego tomorrow. We can make it a weekend. You can be my date to the gala."

"I can't. I have a lot of work to do."

Ona pouted. "You're always working."

"Says the woman leaving for San Diego tomorrow."

"No fair, you know I have to travel. We go where the money is, where the need is."

"It doesn't bother me. Just be real about it. Don't complain when I work."

"We have so little time together. I just—"

"Ona, we go out every Friday night. Make love more than twice a week. What more do you want?"

"I want you to want to be with me."

"I do. I'm here now."

"You're here, but you aren't here. Date night, sex twice a week . . . It's like you're checking off a list. Come to San Diego with me, please."

Ronin maneuvered out of her embrace, rolling on his side to face her. He didn't want to go to San Diego. But the reality was if he didn't go, there'd be hell to pay. When Ona was feeling insecure, she could be volatile. And once she got like that, there was no reasoning with her. Tomorrow was Solis' birthday, and he had a whole evening planned. The last thing he needed was Ona ruining it.

"Okay, you win. I can't come tomorrow, but I'll catch the first flight out Sunday morning. I'll drop the boys with Mom. We'll stay and come back Monday before the boys get out of school."

Ona snuggled closer to Ronin. "It's a compromise, but I'll take it."

Ronin watched Ona trace the outline of his abdominal muscles with her finger. For the first time in what seemed like forever, he noticed the two-carat diamond ring he'd given her the day he proposed. He remembered how long it took him to decide on which ring to get and how excited he was to hear her say yes. Things were different now.

She was right. He wasn't with her.

Chapter 22

"I could get used to this *Pretty Woman* gig." Marlon relaxed on the dressing room love seat, sipping champagne.

"You know she was a prostitute. I'm offended." Solis preened in the mirror.

"Julia Roberts should be offended. She had to work for it." Marlon laughed.

"I hate you. Which one?"

Marlon pointed, "The emerald green strapless."

"The gentleman has a good eye. My dear, with your figure, I could dress you all day. Now let's try this Coco Chanel."

The style consultant unzipped the dresses back. "Oh, dear, what is this? We must work on your foundation garments. Carly, bring the tape! Come now. Out of this. I need to measure you."

Solis raised her arms. "Paul, I'm really only here for a dress."

"Ms. Monroe, I'm here to be sure you have everything you need. You need foundation garments. Excuse me. Carly!" Paul left to find his assistant.

"Marlon, I don't know. Did you see the tag? This is an Armani. The other dress is a Vera Wang. Do you know how much this cost?"

"Yes, and so does Ronin. He clearly doesn't care, and neither should you. Enjoy yourself, Solis. It's your birthday."

"I don't want to take advantage. I'm not a gold digger."

"Solis, have you asked for any of the things he's given you?"

"No."

"Then you're not a gold digger. I can tell you what you won't be, after tonight . . . a virgin."

"Marlon!"

"Girl, in that dress, you could make a gay man straight."

"Shut up, Marlon!"

"Relax, Solis, I'm just messing with you. Ronin loves you. If he didn't, we wouldn't be sitting here in this expensive dress boutique, sipping champagne, trying on dresses we could never afford. And he wouldn't be waiting."

"I know, and I love him too. But I have nothing to offer. I mean, his wife . . . She is . . . it doesn't make sense. Who would choose me over her?"

"Ronin. And any man who spent more than ten minutes with you. Love doesn't make sense. Stop overthinking it. You're worth it."

"I'm back." Paul announced his return with glee. "Arms up. Let's wrap those lovely ladies in something befitting their grandeur. Your panty, Ms. Monroe?"

"Six," Solis replied.

"I'll have Carly set a lingerie table. While you make your selections, I'll steam the Armani and bag it for you. Are we settled on the silver accessories?"

"Yes, we are, thank you. Paul . . ."

"Ms. Monroe?"

"I'll take the Vera Wang too. And the other sling backs. And whatever is on the lingerie table. Oh, and I'll have more champagne too."

"Splendid! I'll see to it. If you'll excuse me." Paul stepped away.

"That a girl! You get dressed. I'm going to make your selections from the lingerie table."

"I can do it myself."

"Yes, you can. But I can make sure the brother gets his monies' worth."

"You're a jerk."

"You know I love you, baby."

"I love you too."

"Get dressed. We still have hair and makeup to do, birthday girl."

*****

The light on Ronin's line began to blink. He pressed the button. "Christopher?"

"We're here, Mr. Jackson. Ms. Monroe is on her way up."

"Thank you, Christopher."

Ronin opened the jewelry box on his desk. Inside, a pair of diamond earrings with a pendant and matching bracelet. He couldn't wait to see Solis' face when he gave them to her. Her smile was his drug of choice.

He heard a soft taping at the door. "Come in. I'm ready to go. I just need to find my—" Ronin couldn't move. Solis was stunning. "Woman, you tempt me beyond reason."

"If you'd prefer, I could just take it all off." Solis winked at him.

"Next birthday, wicked girl."

Ronin came around the desk. He handed her a small pastry box from behind his back. "Open it."

Solis quickly removed the box lid. Inside, a red velvet cupcake from Dulce, complete with a candle.

"You horrible man! Do you know what it took to get into this dress? Let alone to get the eye shadow right. You're going to make me cry."

"One cupcake won't hurt." Ronin lit the candle. "You have to have cake, it's your birthday. Now make a wish and blow out the candle so you can open the rest of your presents."

Solis blew out the candle, barely able to contain her excitement. "There's more?"

"You better believe it. Close your eyes." Solis shut her eyes. Ronin took the pendant out of the box. "Now open them."

"Ronin . . ." Solis teared up.

"Don't give me all the credit. I had a little help from Mr. Smirnov. He is very fond of you."

Solis watched as Ronin put the jewelry on her piece by piece. "Ronin, I will remember this moment as long as I live. Thank you."

"Beautiful women should have beautiful things. I love you. Happy birthday, beautiful. We should get going. I don't want to be late for our reservation. Did you square things with Dahlia?"

"Yes. Are you in the clear with Ona?"

"Good to go." Ronin held out his arm. "Shall we?"

When they reached the parking level, Christopher was waiting.

"Ms. Monroe, I said it before, and I'll say it again, you are a beautiful woman. Happy birthday."

"Thank you, Chrissy. You ain't too bad yourself." Solis stepped into the limo.

"Chrissy? Christopher . . ."

"Mr. Jackson, a woman that fine can call me anything she wants as long as she calls me. I mean no disrespect." Christopher tipped his hat.

Ronin laughed. "None taken." Ronin palmed Christopher's hand with a hundred. "For your discretion."

"Always. Thank you, sir."

Chapter 23

"Why did we buy the boys anything for Christmas when Grandma Charlotte bought them their own personal Toys R Us?" Joi shook her head as she laid the gifts out on the table.

Ona nodded in agreement. "Right. Does she know how much it's going to cost to ship all of this stuff home from Ohio?"

"I don't think she cares. She's just happy to see them. Hand me the wrapping paper."

"She could see them anytime she wants, planes fly in both directions."

"Don't start, Ona. You know how much Mom hates California. Besides, this way, the boys get to play in the snow."

"How on earth did you get Brodie to let you have them for Christmas?"

"I let him off the hook for child support for this month."

"Extortion? That is obscene. What kind of father extorts the mother of his children?"

"One that doesn't give two shits if he sees them or not. It's only going to get worse when Alice has that baby."

"You doing okay with that?"

"It still hurts. I shouldn't care, but . . ."

Ona held her hand. "He betrayed you in the worst way. That kind of pain doesn't heal quickly."

"I know, but I think Marcus wants to get married . . . have kids of our own. How can I do that if I still feel some kind of way about what Brodie did?"

"You love Marcus. If you and Brodie didn't have to co-parent, it'd be easier, but you can't put your life on hold. What are you going to do, wait until the boys are eighteen? If Marcus wants to take up the mantle, let him."

"He's coming here for Christmas. He'll be here the twenty-third."

"You don't think he is going to propose, do you?"

"God no. He wouldn't do it with the boys around. He just wants to meet Mom and spend some time with the boys. When does Ronin get here?"

"Tomorrow."

"You guys doing okay?"

"Yes. We just spent a day in San Diego together. It was fun. I still feel like he's a little distant, but I can pull him in with a little effort."

"Men. Ugh."

"Speaking of . . .look who's calling." Ona answered, "Hey love, how are you?"

"Good. I'm calling to let you know that I won't be coming in tomorrow. The soonest I can get there is the twentieth."

"Ronin, it's Christmas. We always spend Christmas together."

"We are going to spend Christmas together. I'll be there on the twentieth. I just can't get away now," Ronin tried to explain.

"What am I going to tell the boys? That their father would rather work than go with them to their grandparents in Ohio for Christmas?"

"I'll call back and talk to them myself later."

"Ronin, why can't someone else in the firm do whatever it is?" Ona asked, irritated.

"Ona, I'll be there before Christmas."

"Why is it that every time I want to do something to bring this family together, you bail?"

"Bail? Did you come to me before you decided we'd go to Ohio to visit your mother for Christmas? Did you ask me if I had anything to do before you bought the tickets? No, you didn't."

"You just don't want to spend time with me. And you're still trying to avoid Joi."

"This isn't about you or your sister. It's about my job. If you think dogging me out or staying mad at me will get you what you want, don't because it won't."

Ronin hung up. Ona held the phone in disbelief. He wasn't coming.

Charlotte opened the bedroom door. "How's the wrapping coming? I know I over did it, but that's a grandmother's prerogative." Charlotte noticed the girls weren't laughing. "What's wrong?"

"Ronin isn't coming tomorrow." Joi replied.

"No. He'll be here on the twentieth. Mom, I don't know what to do. He's drifting away from me." Ona cried.

"Drifting away? Ona, it's two days."

"I had this whole vacation planned, and he's ruining it."

"Ona, honey, you got to let go a little. If a person feels like they're suffocating, they'll go looking for air. Give the man some space."

"I won't let him do to me and the boys what Daddy did to you, to us."

"Ona, listen to me. Ronin isn't your father. You've got to let it go. I have. Joi has. It's unhealthy."

"Mom . . . he can't leave. I won't let him."

"We shouldn't get ahead of ourselves. Ronin will be here in a couple of days. Maybe a change of scenery and the Christmas spirit will do you both some good. Don't worry, things have a way of working themselves out."

"I should call him back."

"No. No, you shouldn't." Joi exclaimed. "Let him call back like he said."

"What you need is a little retail therapy, get your mind off things." Charlotte smiled.

"I love you, Mom." Ona replied.

"You better because you're paying." Charlotte chuckled.

****

Ronin stood in front of the refrigerator, staring at takeout menus. He'd spent the better part of two days neck deep in contracts for upcoming negotiations and was in desperate need of a break.

The house phone rang. It was Ona, checking up on him. Why else call the home phone?

"You want me to answer that?" Damien asked.

"No, I got it."

Ronin let it ring a few more times and picked up. "Hey, love, you and the boys all right?"

"The boys and I are having a great time. How about you?"

"Reading over boring contracts. You just caught me standing in front of the fridge trying to decide which takeout I'm going to order tonight. What'd you guys do today?"

"I hope you like icicles. The boys don't want to do anything but play in the snow. Mom and I did some last-minute shopping before Christmas. You have any plans for tomorrow?"

"I've got to get through these contracts. Damien and I are going to get together for a few beers. That's about it. Are the boys around?"

Ona called Ronin Jr. and Robert, "Boys, Daddy is on the phone."

Robert spoke first. "Hey, Dad."

"Hey, buddy, is your brother with you?"

"I'm here," Ronin Jr. replied.

"Good. Guys, I wanted to tell you that I'm not going to be there tomorrow. I have some work to finish, and I can't leave yet."

"Are you going to be here for Christmas? You won't miss Santa Claus?" Robert asked, worried.

"I'll be there before Santa gets there. Promise."

Robert broke into a smile. "That's good. Can I go back to my game now? I was beating Ronin. I never beat Ronin."

"Yes, buddy, you can go. What about you, Chief?"

Ronin Jr. waited for Robert to leave before he answered. "First, I'm letting Robert win. He's always crying about losing. Second, if you're going to be here for Christmas, I'm good."

"Thanks for being so understanding, Chief . . . and for letting your brother win for a change. Give your mom back the phone. I'll see you soon."

"Okay. Ronin I wanted to apologize for earlier, I—"

"I got to get back to work. Kiss the boys for me and tell your mother I said hello. I'll see you in a couple of days."

"I love you. Don't forget to bring the other gifts with you."

"I won't. I love you too. Get back to the boys. We'll talk later. Good night."

"Damn, she's checking up on you like that. Fool, why do you even have a home phone?" Damien asked. "Nobody has a home phone anymore."

"I have one just in case. Don't even get me started on Ona. She was trying to apologize for our fight. I wasn't having it. If it weren't for the boys, I'd stay right here . . . and she knows it. That's why she's all sweetness and light all of a sudden."

"Ro, you can't live like this. You need to get a divorce."

"No. Maybe when the boys are older but not now. It would be too traumatic for them . . . especially Robert."

"I'd believe you were worried about my nephews if you weren't having an affair with their babysitter. That's still going on, isn't it? Where is the little Lolita? Thought, for sure, I'd be interrupting . . . again."

"I love my boys. I'm not sleeping with her. Solis' last final is today, and she'll be at the house tomorrow."

"Yet. What do you have planned? Do I need to show up and save you again?"

"I don't know but hanging out at the house is not on the list of activities. Let's go out. Chinese?"

"Steak. You can't buy a reprieve from my Jiminy Cricket routine for noodles."

"Steak it is. Anything to get you to shut up."

*****

"Finals are done!" Iris danced a little jig. "We need to celebrate. Let's do something fun this weekend."

"Why not tonight?" Solis replied.

"Tonight? No one hangs out on a Thursday night. You're so square."

"Better than being obtuse." Solis chuckled.

"Geometry jokes? Definition of square. No, really tomorrow night."

"I'm at the Jacksons' tomorrow, and it's Christmastime, Marlon needs me at the store."

"Liar! Something is going on. The candy store, I buy, but the Jacksons . . . you damn near live over there. You're there more than the store. And your wardrobe has taken a sudden expensive turn for the better. What gives?"

"I'm making a little more money. Aren't you always after me to dress better?"

"Yes, but that requires shopping. Which you hate."

"I found this new thing called the Internet. You buy things, and they bring them to your house. It's great."

"How about this—I'll come with you to the Jacksons' tomorrow? We can watch the boys together. I won't even take a cut. After their parents get home, we'll go out."

"I don't think that's a good idea. I'm not sure Ona would be okay with it. Let's just hang out tonight."

"Call her. Call her right now and ask."

"No. Maybe later. I'll let you know. What do you want to do tonight?"

Solis was a terrible liar. Iris knew it. And Solis knew she knew it, yet she persisted. Solis was hiding something. She'd been keeping something from her for months, but for the life of her, she couldn't figure out what it was. Today she wasn't going accept Solis' excuses.

"Let's see. I want to—" Iris snatched Solis's phone.

"Give it back, Iris!" Solis screamed.

"Ona, here's the number, 555—"

Solis tackled Iris to the ground and took her phone back. "You'll ruin everything!" Solis shouted, crying.

"Ruin what? What's wrong with you?"

"Mr. Jackson. I'm going to see him tomorrow. I can't call Ona because she's out of town with the kids." Solis wiped the tears from her eyes. "You can't say anything . . . to anyone ever. . . Swear it."

"Oh my god, Solis. I swear it," Iris replied, picking herself up off the ground.

"We can't talk about it . . . ever."

"Oh no, you ain't getting off that easy. When, where, what, why, and how? Spill it."

"When, eight months ago. Where, at the candy store. Why? Because he is incredibly sexy, thoughtful, and kind. How, I don't know, it just happened. We met for coffee and just kept meeting."

"And the what?"

"What?"

"Yes, what—what are you doing? Are you sleeping with him?"

"No. I want to. We've come close, but the age thing . . . We're waiting."

"Age?"

"Thirty-nine."

"Thirty-nine! Solis, when I said older, I didn't mean that old. Only you could find a sugar daddy and still be a virgin. Eight months and you didn't tell me?"

"If anyone found out, even by accident . . ."

"I get it, but I'm still mad. We're best friends."

"I just couldn't, Iris."

"Sleepover. I need details. Apparently, you've been living a double life the last eight months."

"Your house or mine?"

"Yours, maybe I'll get a glimpse of Marlon in his birthday suit." Iris bit her lower lip.

Solis rolled her eyes. "Iris, he's gay."

"That's only because he hasn't been with me yet."

"You're incorrigible. My house it is."

Chapter 24

It was Valentine's Day, and Amour et Chocolat was a madhouse. Solis was packing custom orders by the dozen, and Piper was ringing out prepackaged boxes and baskets faster than Marlon and Bobby could restock the shelves.

Focused on the box in front of her, Solis didn't notice the two delivery men enter the store.

"Are you Ms. Solis Monroe?" the first man asked.

"Yes. How may I help you?" Solis looked over the partition. She could tell the man was exhausted, no doubt having the same kind of day she was.

"Miss, these roses are for you."

The second delivery man approached the counter with two dozen ruby red roses.

"For me?" Solis asked, surprised.

"Yes, for you. Where would you like us to put them?"

"Behind the counter here is fine," Solis pointed in the direction of the counter.

The second man put the roses on the back counter, smiling at her. "I can see why someone sent you roses. Will you sign for them?"

"Yes, thank you. Would you gentleman like a sample?"

"I'd love a sample," the first man replied.

Solis handed them both two pieces of candy each. On their way out the door, several customers followed them to see if they had extra flowers for sale.

"Who are they from?" the woman whose box Solis was packing asked.

"A very special someone." Solis blushed.

"Honey, I know you're busy, but you should take a moment to read your card and enjoy your flowers." The woman gave Solis an approving nod.

Solis hurried over to the roses and opened the card.

I know red is overdone. But I was thinking . . . classics never go out of style.

All my love . . . Ronin.

Solis felt her cell vibrate in her pocket. "Ronin, they're beautiful. Thank you. How'd you know they were here?"

"I paid the delivery guys extra to call me when you got them. I'm glad you like them."

"I love them. Red and all."

"I'm sorry you're going to spend the evening watching the boys and not with me."

"No worries. You can make it up to me later. I've got to go. I love you."

"I love you too."

The woman gave Solis a knowing smile. "Someone is in love, I think."

"Desperately. I'm desperately in love with him," Solis answered back.

*****

"I can't believe we're at The Ellington. This place is even rich for our blood," Ona snickered.

"I wanted it to be special," Ronin replied.

"And the Fairmont too. You're earning your gold stars tonight. I'll have to reward you later with a little Valentine surprise."

"I always enjoy the gold-star treatment." Ronin grinned.

"I'm so glad Solis could watch the boys. She's been a godsend. Before we left, she was telling me how busy the store was. She said the lines were out the door, they ran out of candy and had to turn people away. She said her favorite customers are the men who ask her what she likes and then buy it for their wife, girlfriend, or whomever. I cracked up. I don't know how she does it. I'd lose it."

When Ronin didn't respond, Ona could tell he was only half listening.

"Ronin? You know this is our twelfth Valentine's Day."

"No, I didn't. You're much better at keeping up with those type of things than I am."

"If you cared, it'd be easy to remember."

"I do care. Those guys asking Solis what she likes are just a bunch of poor bastards trying not to get their asses handed to them when they get home. I made this reservation two months ago. Does that mean I love you any more than the guy who forgot? It could be the complete opposite. Yet his love and devotion will be questioned and mine won't. Why? Because I remembered? It just doesn't seem fair."

Ona wasn't sure what to say. Ronin's candor and visible irritation surprised her.

"I never looked at it that way. I guess we women should give you guys a break on Valentine's Day. But birthdays and anniversaries are still subject to the same rules. You forget, you're in big trouble."

"Twelve years and two kids later, are you happy?" Ronin asked seriously.

"Of course. I love you and the boys."

"I'm not asking if you love us. I'm asking if you're happy."

"What's the difference? I love my life. I'm happy. Are you?"

"I don't know. Sometimes I wonder if there is more."

"More what? We have everything."

"Do we?" Ronin asked.

"Our life is good. What else do we need?"

Ona was upset. This was not the kind of conversation she expected to have on Valentine's Day. Ronin was always good when it came to romance. Tonight, he was failing miserably. If she didn't know any better, she'd think he was doing it on purpose.

"Nothing. Just forget it. I don't want to ruin our evening. To us." Ronin raised his glass.

"To us." Ona did the same.

"Did you want dessert? Maybe a dessert wine? I know how much you like chocolate mousse. I was thinking chocolate cheesecake."

"I do love chocolate, and you know I never turn down wine. Oh, did I tell you I think Marcus is going to pop the question tonight?"

"So soon?"

"We'd only been dating a year when you proposed."

"Yeah, but the timing was right. I don't know. Marcus is a great guy, but Joi has baggage."

"It's Valentine's Day. Let's have faith in love, if only for tonight, and be happy for them."

"For tonight."

Chapter 25

"What are you up to?" Marlon asked, emptying his pockets on the entry table.

"What all single bitches do on this holiday—get shit-faced and watch movies where some bitch that ain't you gets her man." Dahlia snorted.

Marlon took note of the two wine bottles on the table and the third in her hand. He sighed. After a long day at work, the last thing he needed was a drunk Dahlia.

"Dahlia, three bottles?"

"It doesn't matter, I'm not going anywhere," she slurred back.

Marlon sat down. "I hate this holiday too. The only thing good about it is the amount of money the store brings in."

Dahlia offered Marlon the bottle. Marlon took several large gulps, trying to leave little for Dahlia to finish.

"As always, it was crazy. I couldn't have made it through without Solis. She has a way of dealing with customers that takes the edge off them."

"That's because the assholes are too busy thinking about fucking her to be mad."

"Don't ever say that about Solis again. I don't care how drunk you are."

"I swear you're like her daddy. She doesn't need me. She has you. Where is she?"

"She's babysitting for the Jacksons tonight. She promised the boys she'd come. They really love her."

"Everyone really loves her. She's so loveable, it makes me sick."

"Do you hear yourself? She's your daughter."

A sadness washed over Dahlia's face. "I'm a horrible mother."

"You could be better if you tried."

"Be better? My mother hated me . . . You don't get it."

"Dahlia, my mother is crack whore who I've seen maybe ten times since CPS picked me up damn near twenty years ago. What's for me to get?"

"Keyva tried, Darrell just . . . You don't understand what it was like."

"No? You forget, Solis and I lived with Ulayla too. Solis wasn't old enough to remember everything; but she remembers enough. Solis is your daughter. Be her mother. You can start by taking your ass to bed. I don't want Solis to come home and find you like this."

"Wouldn't be the first time." Dahlia laughed.

Dahlia got up and almost fell. Marlon caught her and half carried, half walked her to her room. Dahlia was asleep before her head hit the pillow.

Marlon went back to the living room and cleaned up Dahlia's drunken pity party. Afterward, he got the sub sandwich, chips, and beer he bought on the way home and crashed on the couch.

He wasn't shocked by anything Dahlia said. Some mothers live vicariously through their daughters, others take pride in their accomplishments, and still others resent and envy them, seeing their lives as a theft of their own. Dahlia fell into the last group as did Marie and Ulayla. But unlike them, Dahlia didn't abandon Solis. Damaged as she was, it gave him hope that one day Dahlia could be better.

*****

Ona removed her coat. "Is that music? The boys should be in bed."

"Calm down, Ona. It's Saturday night. If the boys are still up, it doesn't matter. Is that cookies I smell?"

Ronin and Ona followed the sounds and aromas to their source. In the kitchen, they found Solis and the boys dancing and singing at the top of their lungs.

"Is that Otis Redding?" Ona asked.

"Yes. Yes, it is. I didn't know Ronin Jr. could dance like that," Ronin replied, amused.

Solis noticed the two standing in the doorway and stopped the music. "You're home. I wasn't expecting you until tomorrow."

"I can see that. I thought the boys would be in bed by now. Are those cookies?" Ona glared at Solis.

"I promised the boys I'd make them something special tonight. Valentine cookies were just something fun and tasty. I thought just once wouldn't hurt," Solis explained.

Oblivious, Robert hit the last track on the iPod. "Daddy, listen!"

"Come on, Dad, dance with us!" Ronin Jr. dragged Ronin into the kitchen. Solis joined in, feeling the tension dissipate.

"Mommy, you too. Come dance with us," Robert called to Ona.

Ona didn't move. An icy feeling washed over her. Ronin had been sullen and distant all night. Now here with Solis and the boys, he had come alive. She shut off the music.

"Why'd you do that?" Ronin asked Ona.

"It's bedtime," Ona replied flatly.

"Mommy, please let us stay up a little longer. Please?" Ronin Jr. pleaded.

"No. It's bedtime. Do not ask again. Go."

"Solis, can you still read us a story and tuck us in?" Robert asked sadly, unaware of the fuel his request was adding to what was already primed to be an epic explosion.

Solis moved quickly to intervene. "Robert, you and Ronin do as your mother asked. If it's okay with Mommy, when I'm done cleaning up, I'll come say good night. Make sure you brush your teeth for two minutes, tops and bottoms."

"Solis go upstairs with the boys. Read them their story and tuck them in." Ronin ordered. "Ona and I will clean up down here."

Ona wanted to say no. She wanted to scream no. Ronin's face told her not to.

"Yes!" Ronin Jr. and Robert shouted in unison.

"Hush," Solis scolded them and led them out of the kitchen.

"Are you kidding me? What the hell is wrong with you?" Ronin whispered angrily.

"What's wrong with me? What's wrong with you? We're supposed to be in a suite making love, but instead, we're here."

"You're mad at me. Don't take it out on the boys and Solis."

"Solis did not follow my instructions. I set rules for a reason. I expect them to be followed. Why didn't you support me just now?"

"Support you? They stayed up past their bedtime making cookies. Why on earth would you have a problem with that? Solis is doing her job. The boys are happy. Why can't you see that?"

"I don't want to talk about this anymore."

Ona stormed off. She could see it, and she didn't like it.

*****

About a half-hour later; Solis came into the kitchen. "The boys are down. Teeth brushed, stories read, and tucked in their beds. They were asleep before I finished the chapter. I think all our dancing tired them out. Since you guys are home, I you won't need me to stay. Ronin, can you take me home?" Solis asked.

"No. I'll take you home." Ona gestured toward the door.

"Let me get my things." Solis gathered her bags and followed Ona to the car.

Ona was furious. Ronin too. Solis didn't know what happened, but it was clear dinner didn't go well. If the atmosphere in the house was tense, the mood in the car was frigid.

"You're quite the charmer. Every man in my house is enamored with you."

Jealousy. Solis wasn't surprised; Ona was jealous by nature. But this was different. Something in the evening's events brought about a change; Ona now viewed her as a threat.

"It's the Mary Poppins effect. I come in and do all the fun stuff. You're Mom. You do the mom stuff. Believe me, they want you, not me. I'm sorry. I know the boys' bedtime, and I shouldn't have let them stay up or made them cookies without your permission."

"You got Ronin Jr. to dance and sing. He's always so quiet."

"That wasn't hard. Who can resist Ottis Redding? Ronin is plenty talkative if you're talking something, he's interested in. He really likes to read. I try to read the books he's reading, if I haven't read them already. It's always more fun to read a book when you have someone to talk to about it."

"You've gotten to know the boys well. I'm surprised you have time with school and work."

"Ronin is in the fourth grade. We're talking about Lemony Snicket, not Tolstoy. And Robert? Robert is an Energizer Bunny with no off switch. Just keep him moving and make it fun."

"Tolstoy? You've read Tolstoy?"

"Yes. I don't recommend it. Unless you're out of Xanax."

Solis hoped her levity would lighten Ona's mood. To her surprise, it did.

"I owe you an apology, Solis. I was incredibly rude. I'm sorry."

"I understand. I tend to get a little snippy when things don't go as planned. Did you still want me back next week?"

"Yes, and if you want to push bedtime back a little, I'm okay with that." Ona smiled.

"I won't do it too often. Promise."

"Is this it?" Ona pointed toward the brick condo on the corner.

"Yup. You can let me out here. Good night, Ona."

"Wait, did we pay you?"

"Give it to me next time. Good night."

Solis left as quickly as she could without making it obvious, she was in a hurry to get away. No amount of money was worth spending another minute in the car with Ona. The moment Ona drove away, Solis called Ronin.

"Ronin, what the hell did you do? Do you have any idea how awkward it was riding in a car with your angry wife?"

"Forgive me. Dinner was a disaster. I didn't want to be there, and I didn't do a good job of hiding it. I apologized. She wouldn't let it go. I said to hell with it and insisted we go home."

"I'd have been pissed at you too. Ronin, are you an idiot? She's your wife. It was one night, and you couldn't keep it together? Then you challenge her in front of me? I thought she was going to fire me on the spot. Maybe I should quit."

"Yes, I'm an idiot. And no, you aren't quitting. The boys would be crushed. Our problems are our problems, not yours and the boys. I love you, Solis. Do you know that?"

"I love you too. Now fix this. Good night."

Chapter 26

"Doesn't this remind you of our honeymoon in Mexico? The view from this veranda is amazing."

"If it weren't for the veranda, we would've seen little, if any, of Mexico."

"We should go again. A short trip, just a few days."

It took a lot of work to repair things between the two of them after Valentine's Day, but he'd done it. Ona was happy and feeling secure in their relationship again. The problem? He wasn't. If anything, he was growing more dissatisfied by the day. The last thing he wanted was a romantic weekend getaway.

"I'm really busy at work right now. It'd be hard to get away. And then there's the boys."

"Joi can hold down the fort without me. I'm sure Byron wouldn't mind covering for you. We can leave the boys with your mother."

He wasn't getting out of it. Everything she said was true. The trip was completely doable. To continue to resist would only upset her and undo all his hard work.

"Okay, but instead of leaving the boys, we should bring them with us."

"I was thinking just us."

"I was thinking it's been a while since we went anywhere as a family. Spring break is in a few weeks."

"How are we supposed to spend time together with the boys underfoot?"

"We can find one of those resorts that is family-friendly and rent a suite. We could hire a nanny while we're there. That way, we can spend time with the boys and still have alone time with each other."

"A nanny? Seriously? I don't know if the boys would be comfortable in the care of just anyone."

"Let's take Solis."

"Solis?"

"Why not? The boys would have a great time with her. We could come and go as we please and still fit in some quality time with the boys. It's perfect."

"Do you think Solis would do it? Would her mother be okay with it?"

"I don't see why not. We can ask her when we get home tonight. You can give her mom a call in the morning. Great! I'm excited already. I'm glad you suggested it."

"Me too."

It was obvious Ona wasn't keen on the idea of taking Solis and the boys on vacation with them, but he was excited about the idea. Spending time with the boys would be fun, and he was sure he could fit some quality time in with Solis too. Now all he had to do was convince Solis.

*****

"You're home." Solis got up from the couch. "I'll get my things. Ona, I'm ready to go whenever you are."

"Wait, Ona and I have something to ask you. We're thinking about taking a quick little vacation. Would you mind watching the boys?" Ronin asked.

"Of course not. I'd love too. When?"

"We'd all leave for México next month, over spring break."

"All of us?"

"Yes. You'd come with us."

"Only if you want to," Ona added. "If you have other plans, we'd understand. I wouldn't want to spend my spring break babysitting."

"It'd only be for a week. You'd have time to do your own thing when the boys are with us."

Solis studied Ona. There was no way this was her idea. On the surface everything appeared good between the two of them, but Solis knew better. Ona was still jealous and very suspicious of her. Ronin was playing with fire.

"But you'd still be with the boys a lot of the time," Ona added.

Ona was begging Solis to say no. And Solis knew she should. But the idea of a spring break trip to Mexico was too good to resist, and she could tell Ronin really wanted her to go.

"I don't mind. I'd be working if I stayed here anyway. I need to talk to Dahlia and Marlon. Since its spring break, it shouldn't be a problem?"

"Talk to them. If they green light it. Ona will call her with all the details as soon as I make them."

Solis could see the lava roiling just beneath Ona's skin. She hadn't surrendered to the idea. It wasn't over.

"Ona, I think Robert is coming down with something. He wasn't the Energizer Bunny I've come to love. I checked his temperature. He's warm but no fever. We hung out on the couch mostly and watched *Peter Pan* again."

"Thank you for taking care of him and for watching *Peter Pan* for the hundredth time."

"Captain Hook never gets old. But I'm to try and get him to watch *Hook*. Change it up a bit."

"Good plan. I'm going to check on him. Ronin will take you home tonight. See you next week."

Chapter 27

"I can't believe you got me at IHOP this damn early." Marlon yawned.

"It's only eight. Besides, it's your birthday, and you love pancakes."

"I love sleep more."

"I've got the whole day planned. We have spa appointments at ten."

"Solis, did you forget I have a store to run?"

"Piper and Bobby are running the ship with a temp from corporate. You can't use work as an excuse."

"What?"

"Surprise! Happy birthday!" Iris sat down at the table.

"Oh hell, no! It's too damn early for Iris," Marlon grumbled.

"Sexy, it's never too early for me." Iris winked.

Marlon waved the server down. "Coffee, please. Black."

Iris raised her hand. "Me too, with cream and sugar. Thank you. Now tell me why I'm here this early in the morning."

"Last night, Ronin asked me to go with the family to Mexico for spring break as the nanny."

"He's taking you to Mexico?" Iris asked, surprised.

"No, Iris. The family is going to Mexico. I'm going with them. There's a difference."

"Solis, you are too smart to be so dumb," Iris quipped.

"I'll have to swallow my tongue after I say this, but Iris is right. He's taking you to Mexico. His family . . . is a cover."

"You guys, this isn't a romantic getaway. It's a family vacation. I'll be with the boys most of the time."

"Yeah, and you don't think he'll find time to work in a little 'Solis' on the beach?" Iris scoffed.

"His wife agreed to this?" Marlon asked.

"Reluctantly. I can tell she's isn't happy about the idea."

"She shouldn't be. She's an idiot. I'd cancel the whole trip."

"I agree with Marlon. But Mexico for spring break, we've got to go shopping. I'm thinking of a few bikinis that'll make sure you leave Mexico a new woman. I'm sure there's a pool boy or two on deck."

"First, random pool boys . . . ew. Second, this isn't *Bay Watch*. I'm the nanny. Third, I'm not legal . . . Remember?"

"So what? It isn't like you're going to tell anyone. And if anyone gets ideas, just do what I do—deny it. Unless they catch you doing it, they can't prove anything. Marlon, tell me I'm wrong." Iris sipped her coffee.

"Again, though it pains me . . . Iris is right."

"Well, it may not happen if I can't convince Dahlia to let me go. Do you think she'll go along?"

"Dahlia? She'll say no at first. She always does. It's reflex. I'll give her all the reasons why she is being unreasonable. Get on her case. She'll cave."

"Marlon, you think she'll come home a virgin?" Iris grinned.

"Not a chance." Marlon laughed.

"You guys are awful. Really awful. I'm glad you find my sex life so entertaining." Solis laughed.

Chapter 28

Ona had every moment of the trip planned, the family activities and their alone time. Solis fell in lock step with Ona's daily agendas. She made sure the boys did everything on the schedule, right down to eating and sleeping. The Ona dictatorship was in full effect. But after three days, Ronin decided to call an end to it.

Today he insisted Ona take the boys for the afternoon and give Solis some time off. The boys were good kids, but even he wouldn't want to be stuck with them twenty-four hours a day, paid or not.

Ona demanded he come with them. When he refused, she tried to guilt him into going with them. When the guilt trip didn't work, Ona was furious. He didn't care. He held his ground. Truthfully, it wasn't just about spending time with Solis. He needed some down time. All family, all wife, all the time was wearing on him.

"Solis, only you would come to paradise and read a book."

Solis jumped, startled. "Ronin, I didn't know you were still here. I thought you'd be off with Ona and the boys. It's on the schedule."

"Nope."

"What'd you do? Does Ona know you're here?"

Ronin lifted her off the chair and kissed her. What little resistance she gave, he broke down by deepening the kiss. He sat down and reclined on the chaise with Solis in his arms.

"You're going to get us both killed. Do you know what Ona will do if she catches you here?"

"No more talk about Ona. What's this?" Ronin took the book from her hand. "*The Count of Monte Cristo.* Wow. You like this?"

"It's on my list. I want to read all the classics."

"Aren't you a little young to have a list?"

"I don't think so. I started making a list of things I wanted to do in life when I was nine. My fourth-grade teacher bought me a journal, that's what started it."

"Tell me, what else is on your list?"

"I want to travel to as many places as I can. I want to live abroad. I want to learn at least two languages other than my own. I want to fall madly in love. What about you? What's on your list?"

"Nothing, I guess. I wanted to go to a college and study law. I did. I wanted to work for a prestigious law firm. I did. I wanted to start my own law firm. I did. I wanted a wife and kids. I have them. I wanted to make a lot of money. I do. I guess I've done everything on my list."

"Wife, check. Babies, check. Money, check. Good job, check. No wonder you are unhappy. You need a new list."

Ronin wrapped his arms around her. "You're an amazing woman, Solis. Is there any room on your list for me?"

Solis relaxed into him. "I said I wanted to fall madly in love, didn't I?"

"You love me?" Ronin smiled.

"Yes. Very much."

"We've never really talked about it, but why don't you care that I'm so much older than you? I have two kids and a wife. Don't you want someone younger with fewer obligations?"

"A better question is, why are you with me? You have a beautiful, accomplished, albeit tyrannical wife and two wonderful boys"

"It isn't enough."

"And I am? Why don't you want someone older with more to offer?"

"Solis, I love you. You make me happy. For me, that is enough."

"You sure about that?"

Ronin kissed her again. "Yes, I am."

"Good. I'd love to stay here like this, but you should go. We don't know how long Ona is going to be gone."

"They're going to a children's snorkeling class. We have some time. You hungry?"

"The shrimp tacos are amazing."

"Shrimp tacos it is."

Chapter 29

Ronin sat at the bar, blood boiling. He'd spent the last hour watching Solis dance with other men, teenagers really. Friday and Saturday nights, the resort held dance parties for teenagers, and Ona encouraged Solis to go. He wouldn't have let her go; it didn't matter that they were at resort. México was still a foreign country, and they didn't know anyone who would be there. Ona fought it, but he insisted on going down to the beach to chaperone.

"¿La joven es muy hermosa, sí?" the bartender asked as he served Ronin his third drink.

"What?" Ronin asked.

"The young lady is very beautiful, yes?" He repeated the question.

"Yes," Ronin answered.

"Creo que el caballero es en el amor."

"In love? I'm married, and she is very young." Ronin couldn't believe he just said those words aloud and to a stranger. He realized he may have had one too many.

The bartender poured him another drink. Ronin pushed the drink away.

"No mas. Café por favor. ¿Como se llama?"

"Miguel. Young, but not too young, I think. As for your wife, ¿*Los hombres estarán los hombres, no?*" Miguel smiled.

"*Sí*, Miguel, men will be men, *pero las esposas serán esposas.*"

"Yes, wives will be wives." Miguel laughed. "Where did you learn Spanish?"

"I spent a year abroad in Cuba when I was in college."

"*Bueno*. Then you will understand when I say *las cabañas están muy privado en esta hora de la noche*. I can get one for you."

Ronin turned back to the party. Solis was making her way up the steps toward him. He tossed back the unfinished shot of tequila and handed Miguel a hundred dollars. "Make it very private."

"Sí señor," Miguel answered with a smile. "Cabana 5."

Ronin met Solis at the top of the stairs. "You ready to go back."

"Ronin, does Ona know you're here?"

"Yes. I told her I was coming to chaperone."

"She believed that?"

"I can be very persuasive. I persuade people for a living. Remember?"

They walked past the pool toward the cabanas on the deck. When Solis thought they were alone, she stopped.

"What's wrong with you? I've never seen you like this, agitated . . . reckless. You've been this way since we got here. I'm surprised Ona hasn't noticed."

"Solis I—" In one motion, Ronin swallowed her mouth, taking all of it in his, and backed her into the cabana. The feel of her in his arms was more than he could take.

He slipped the bikini top from her shoulders. The sight of Solis' bare breast made him stop breathing. He fell to his knees at her feet.

"Go. Please go," Ronin begged, still fighting the battle he'd lost the day he walked into Amour et Chocolat for the second time.

Solis nervously placed his hands on her breast. She untied her sarong and the strings on her bikini bottom and let them fall to the floor between her legs.

"Ronin," she whispered quietly.

"God, you're beautiful."

Ronin carried her to the cabana's large couch. He took his time, licking and tugging at her breast, slowly making his way down the length of her body. Solis' trembling slowly gave way to moans of pleasure. Gently, he placed a hand between her legs, parting them. Solis froze and tried to pull away.

"Trust me," Ronin breathed.

Solis relaxed and opened to him timidly. With a practiced tongue, he began a slow rhythmic caress. To keep her, he wrapped his hands around her hips, pinning her in place.

"Please," Solis pleaded.

Ronin took her with force. Solis cried out at the fullness that came when he entered her.

She covered her face and mouth with her hands. Ronin pulled them away, holding them down on either side of her head.

"No. I want to see your face."

He quickened the pace and power of his stroke; all control lost. Solis arched her back, and he watched the pleasure wash over her face. He wanted more, but he knew it wouldn't be long before more time passed than could easily be explained. He let go and collapsed on top of her.

Ronin moved to lie beside her. Solis rolled over and put her back to him. A fear like he had never known gripped him. "Solis, are you okay? Please talk to me."

"I'm fine. A little embarrassed."

"Solis listen to me. You have done nothing to be ashamed of."

"I know. I'm not a child. I said yes. I wanted to do it. I wanted to be with you."

"It doesn't matter. I should've said no. We can't do this again. Understand?"

"I understand. I have to go." Solis slipped from his embrace. She wrapped herself in the sarong and picked up the pieces of her suit.

"Solis, I don't want you to think—"

"Think what? That you used me for sex?"

Her words hit him like a slug to the chest. "Please tell me you don't think that. Please."

"I have to go. Ona will be looking for me." Solis opened the curtain and left.

Ronin sat in the cabana alone. The scent of Solis surrounded him, clouding his thoughts. She was a virgin; the scarlet proof lay beside him. He'd taken her virginity, panicked, and sent her packing.

Ronin put on his pants and grabbed his shirt. Miguel greeted him when he stepped out of the cabana.

"¿Necesitas algo más, señor?

Ronin took several large bills out of his wallet and gave them to Miguel.

"No. Make this look like it never happened. *Sírveme un trago.* Make it two."

"¿Cerveza?"

"No, something stronger. And Miguel . . . *mi esposa* . . ."

"No hay problema Señor Ronin. Silencio es oro."

"Gracias."

*****

Solis managed to make it past Ona without issue. She'd put her suit back on and fixed her hair in one of the pool houses before she went back to the room. The only thing she had to explain was why Ronin wasn't with her. Angry, she took great pleasure telling Ona that he wasn't chaperoning but getting drunk at the bar the whole time.

Solis ran a bath. She was sore. She didn't need experience to know that Ronin was a larger man than most.

It wasn't like she thought it would be the first time. It wasn't the pain but the lack of tenderness. Ronin didn't make love to her. It was lust, not love.

Solis slid beneath the carpet of bubbles, questions weighing heavy on her heart. Did Ronin love her? Is that all he wanted? Was it all a lie?

*****

It was one in the morning before Ronin made it back to the suite. Ona was waiting.

"Where have you been?"

"Did Solis make it back okay?" Ronin asked, avoiding her question.

"Yes, she did. Can't say the same for you."

Ona's tone said it all. She was mad. He was too drunk and disgusted with himself to care. He'd spent the better part of the last hour trying to come up with a good story. In the end, he decided to state the obvious. He was drunk.

"I was at the bar. I lost track of time and tequila."

"I'd go off on you, but the hangover you'll have tomorrow should be punishment enough."

Ronin waved her off. "I'm going to bed."

"No. I'm going to bed. You're going to the couch."

"Can I at least take a shower in this five-thousand-dollars-a-week suite I paid for?" Ronin shouted.

"Keep your voice down. The boys are asleep. You can take a shower in their room." Ona closed the bedroom door.

In his inebriated and frantic state of mind, the fear of losing Solis or having hurt her was sobering. He desperately wanted to apologize, to tell her that he loved her and would never treat her that way again. But there would be no explaining coming out of her room in the wee hours of the morning should he get caught. It would have to wait.

Ronin took a pillow, crashed on the couch, and waited for the alcohol to do its work.

Chapter 30

"Where are the boys?" Ronin sat straight up, immediately regretting the decision.

"Solis got them up early. They went for breakfast and on an adventure."

"What's on your agenda today?"

"I'm going to get lost in the local market. You should come. We can meet up with the boys and Solis for lunch. Later we can all go to the beach."

"It's the least I can do after last night."

Ona kissed him and gently. "I may have overreacted a bit. The boys and Solis are gone. Let me make it up to you."

"I'm sorry, baby. I'm too hungover for this. I haven't even cleaned up from last night. Maybe you should go without me. I can meet up with you guys later."

"Seriously?" Ona was incredulous.

The last thing Ronin needed this morning was another argument. He tried to soften the sting of his rejection. "Ona, baby, you know I love you. I'd love to have you like that. I don't feel well. Can I make it up to you later, when I can reciprocate?"

"Ronin, the whole reason we brought the boys and Solis was so that we could spend quality time with the boys and each other. Since we got here, you've successfully managed to avoid doing both." Ona grabbed her bag. "Sober up and meet us at the beach later." Ona slammed the door as she left.

Ronin fell back on the couch, head pounding. Being hungover was the least of his problems. Ona was angry. He would have to deal with her later. Right now, Solis needed his attention more. He knew she got up early to avoid him. And if she was avoiding him, she was not okay.

*****

Solis and Ona sat on the beach together, the boys playing in the sand a few feet away. Ona could tell Solis had something on her mind. She wasn't herself.

"Is he that cute?" Ona asked.

"Who?"

"The boy you've been daydreaming about for the last hour. Did you meet him at the party last night?"

"No. I was just thinking about my ex-boyfriend."

"Ex-boyfriend?"

"He was a senior last year. He left for college this fall. It wouldn't have worked. *Liar.*"

"I'm sure there are a lot of other young men out there. You're a very pretty girl."

"That's the problem."

"I've never heard any young woman think being pretty was a problem."

"Boys aren't really interested in me. They are only interested in being seen with me or having sex with me. And frankly, not to be a snob, but most boys my age are kind of dumb."

"I see. I'm sure there must be at least one boy who isn't just interested in sex or a complete knuckle-dragger. Admittedly, at your age, they may be few and far between," Ona said with a chuckle.

"There is one. He's my cousin, and he is gay."

"That definitely complicates things." Ona laughed. "I'm going to go help the boys with their castles. Take the rest of the day off."

"That would be great. Thank you. I was thinking about hitting the spa. Maybe do a little souvenir hunting for Iris, Marlon, and Dahlia."

"Sounds good. I'll see you at dinner."

*****

"Daddy! See the castles we built. Come see! Come see!" Robert squealed with joy.

"Here I come!" Ronin shouted back, walking up the beach.

"Feeling better?" Ona smiled up at him.

"That nap really did the trick. Where's Solis?"

"I gave Solis the afternoon off. She seemed a little upset."

"Is she okay?" Ronin asked, trying not to seem too worried.

"Boy trouble. An ex. We talked. Solis is a very bright girl. I feel bad for her. It's the ignorance of youth that makes it such bliss."

An ex? It was worse than he thought. Ona didn't know it, but he did. Solis was talking about him. She wasn't in the suite this morning, and she'd managed to get Ona to give her the day off. He needed to do damage control and quick. But for now, he'd have to build sandcastles.

"Dad dig more. Make the moat deeper so the water won't wash the castle away," Ronin Jr. interrupted their conversation.

"If I dig any deeper, the castle will fall in," Ronin tried to explain without success.

"Robert, you get more water. Mommy, you are digging in the wrong spot," Ronin continued to give orders, frustrated by their lack of zeal.

"Are you sure you wouldn't rather be in high school?" Ona whispered.

"I'll let you know after little Napoleon finishes telling me how to build a sandcastle."

"I think it is time to redirect some of this energy. We've gotten too serious about building this castle, maybe we should take a fun break. Why don't you boys go hang out in the surf? Mommy will stay here with our things and watch you. Okay?"

"Boys, I think Mommy has a great idea. It's time we got on those boogie boards."

Chapter 31

Miguel waved to Ronin from the patio. "Señor sus hijos y la joven están en la piscina pequeña."

"Gracias." Ronin raised his hand in acknowledgment.

Quite the gamesmen, Solis managed to avoid any significant contact between them since she'd left the cabana two nights ago. With Ona at the spa, Solis would be alone with the boys, and they could talk.

Solis sat poolside in a sexy black one-piece suit circa 1950, complete with Audrey Hepburn sunglasses and wide brim sun hat. He loved her classic style; like everything about her, it was unique.

"Hello, Solis." Ronin sat beside her.

Solis didn't acknowledge him. She stared straight ahead, pretending not to see him.

"Solis."

"Mr. Jackson, the boys will be so excited. Boys, look who's here."

"Mr. Jackson? It's Mr. Jackson now?"

"Daddy, come swim with us?" Robert asked.

"No, buddy, I'm going to hang out on the edge here with Solis and watch you swim."

"We're not alone," Solis replied, keeping her back to him. "Do I even need to ask where your wife is?"

"She took your advice and hit the spa."

"My advice. I see."

"Solis, I'm sorry."

"I am not Ona. I don't need you to come groveling to me to make me feel better. Don't tell me you're sorry. Or that you were drunk. Or that I was a mistake. Or any other lame excuse. It just cheapens it and cheapens me."

"Solis Monroe, you could never be a mistake."

"Really? Because it sure doesn't feel that way."

Ronin moved closer to her. "Solis look at me. Please forgive me. I love you."

"Boys let's get out of the pool. We won't have time to clean up before dinner if we don't get going."

"Solis. I know you're angry and hurt—"

"Leave me alone, Ronin. Go find your wife."

*****

Ronin stood at the edge of the bed, a sleeping Solis in front of him. He was taking huge risk, but she'd driven him to it. She'd avoided him all day by pushing him off on Ona or keeping the boys underfoot. It was killing him. They left tomorrow, and there was no way he was going to let her walk off the plane and out of his life.

He whispered, "Solis."

Solis sat straight up. "What are you doing here?"

"I'm here to do what I should've done the first time."

"Get out! Get out before Ona finds you here."

Ronin yanked the blanket from her. "Don't worry about Ona. Come here."

"No. Get out!" Solis scurried toward the headboard.

Ronin grabbed her ankles and drug her beneath him. "I love you. I will never hurt you again. Say you believe me."

"No."

Ronin studied Solis' face. She was angry, but there was something else; the same something he'd seen at the drive-in, the same something he'd felt in the living room.

Ronin kissed her hard. She fought him for a moment but gave in.

"Say you believe me."

"I believe you," Solis answered breathless.

He gazed down at her. It was back, the anger and hurt in her eyes replaced by the liquid heat of desire.

Ronin made quick work of her clothing and his own. He came to rest between her legs. He felt her body tense in anticipation. She was bracing for pain. Guilt flooded him. He'd hurt her the first time.

"Relax. Not like last time. I promise."

Ronin sheathed himself inside her slowly, giving her time to settle around him. He began a slow push, encouraging her to rock with him, letting her dictate his depth and speed. He caressed her gently, raising the temperature of her skin with each touch of his tongue. Solis wrapped her legs around his waist, forcing him deeper, rocking against him. He wanted to prolong her pleasure, make her beg for release, but there wasn't time. Solis began to shake, his name escaping her lips. Ronin brought himself to climax behind her, careful to keep his passions in check. He didn't want this to be the carnal assault he'd visited upon her the first time.

"Did I hurt you?"

"No." Solis blushed. "I love you, Ronin."

"I love you too. I have to go. Next time, we'll take our time. I won't have to leave."

Ronin kissed her on the forehead. "Good night."

Chapter 32

Damien stepped off the elevator. "Man, I can't believe you're forty. I don't know what's worse—you turning forty or the fact that I'm right behind you."

"Trust me, being forty is worse. Now how long are you supposed to hang around to ensure I make it home for my surprise party?"

"I knew you knew. I told Ona we'd never surprise you. I'm under strict orders to bring you home by six."

"I have a client coming at two thirty. Swing by and get me about four or so."

"A new client?"

"Maybe. SMM & Associates. Have you ever heard of them?"

"No."

Ronin opened the door to his office. Solis was sitting on his desk, in cranberry lace bra and matching boy short.

"Happy birthday, Mr. Jackson." Solis smiled, tickled by his response.

"Mercy." Damien muttered under his breath.

"Damien, would you leave us alone for a while? I promise you'll have him in time to get him home by six."

Damien shook his head. Ronin ignored his disapproval and closed the door.

"Solis, I have a meeting with a potential client in thirty minutes."

"SMM & Associates." Solis' eyes sparkled with mischief.

"How'd you know?"

"I'm the CEO of Solis Marie Monroe & Associates."

Ronin fought back a smile. This was a side of Solis he hadn't seen before. Curious where she'd take it, he played along.

"Ms. Monroe, you have my full and undivided attention. What is it I can do for you?" Ronin sat down in the large chair behind his desk, taking off his shirt and shoes.

"I'd like to discuss a merger. You do work in mergers and acquisitions?"

"I do. Who were you considering a merger with?"

"I was thinking of a merger with the Jackson firm. Have you heard of them?"

"I'm familiar with the firm. Do you trust me to handle the merger?"

Ronin took off his pants, struggling restrain himself. He didn't want to hurt her, but the hunger she'd aroused in him was all-consuming.

"Yes."

"Are you sure? I only ask because today the Jackson firm is interested in a hostile takeover."

"How hostile?"

For a moment, he thought he might let her off the hook, but she started the game, and he was going to finish it. Ronin cleared the desk with one hand and put Solis on it with the other. He tore everything from her body, pulling her back into the chair, and set her in his lap. Wet and wanting, Solis slid down the length of him until they were one.

"Don't close your eyes." Ronin spoke in a hushed voice.

Solis fixed her gaze on him. Ronin ran his fingers through her hair, taking one of her breasts in his mouth, slowly molesting it with his tongue. He followed the curve of her back with his hands, grabbing her ass firmly and pulling her up so they would be face-to-face. He kissed her face softly, licking her lips, sucking and tugging at them as he went. Solis responded with kisses of her own.

"I could keep you like this. Here in my arms forever. Just like this. God, I love you, Solis."

And he did, slowly bringing her to the edge of release, only to deny her. Solis clung to him, riding him ever harder in search of the climax she desperately needed.

"Please, please," Solis pleaded.

"You are mine. Say it."

"I am yours, Ronin. I am. I am."

"And I am yours. I love you, Solis."

Ronin drove in deep. Solis began to shake violently as the orgasm grew. She let out a primal scream, a mixture of pain and pleasure. Afraid he might hurt her, Ronin let go with an exhausted growl of his own. Solis collapsed in his arms.

"Solis," he called her name softly.

"It's never been like that. I wanted you. I can't even describe it."

"It's absolutely okay to like sex. It's okay to want me. I want you more than you know."

Ronin's cell phone rang. It was Ona. He silenced it and sent the call to voice mail.

"It's getting late. I'm supposed to watch the boys tonight during your party. Ona wants me there before six."

No sooner than the words left her lips, Solis' phone lit up. "Ona."

"What does she want?" Ronin asked, irritated by her interruption.

Solis skimmed the text. "She wants me there earlier. Ronin Jr. and Robert are getting in the way." Solis put the phone down and moved to get up.

Ronin grabbed her. "Don't go. Stay."

"Ronin, I can't. We can't. Ona is already suspicious, and if we're both late . . ." Solis kissed him on the forehead. "We can finish this later. Tomorrow afternoon, maybe? Oh, before I forget, I have something for you."

Solis pulled a gift, beautifully wrapped in black paper with a silver ribbon, from underneath the desk.

"Happy birthday! Finding a gift for a man who has everything is hard, but I remembered one thing you don't have."

"What's this?" Ronin asked, intrigued.

"If you want to know what it is, open it."

Ronin opened the box. It was a leather journal with the words The List embossed on the front.

"There's more."

Ronin opened the journal. On the inside cover was a note.

Make a list of those things you can look back on
when you're old and feel like you've lived.
You will always be on my list.
All my love . . . Solis

Ronin was quiet.

"You don't like it. I can get you something else," Solis offered, disappointed.

"No. I don't want another gift. If I never got another gift, it wouldn't matter. This gift is enough." Ronin kissed her long and slow. "I am desperately in love with you, Solis Marie Monroe, and I cannot live without you."

"You'll never have to. I need to get going. I have to go home and wash the evidence of our tryst away before I see Ona."

Ronin picked up his desk phone. "Christopher. Hey. Please take Ms. Monroe home and anywhere else she needs to go. If need be, wait for her. Charge the trip to the card on file. Don't forget your tip."

Damien knocked on the door. "Ronin. Ona is blowing up my phone. We really should get going."

Solis opened the door. "You don't have to talk through the door. I'm on my way out. He's all yours just like I promised. I'll see you boys at the party."

Damien surveyed the damage. "Man, what the hell did you do?"

"Gentlemen don't tell. I'll come in tomorrow and take care of this. Let's go. I got to run by your house and clean up."

"Ro, I'm not cool with this. What's the end game with this girl? You can't marry her. Hell, you're old enough to be her dad."

"I'm going to divorce Ona."

"You're insane. Did she cast a spell on you or some shit? She's seventeen, Ro. Sexing her is one thing. Leaving your wife and kids for her is something else."

"I know how old she is. I don't care. I need her."

"Ro, you're forty. Not some pussy-whipped teenager."

"I understand what you're saying. I do. It's completely irrational, selfish, and self-destructive. I tell myself that every day . . . all day. I think about leaving her, going back to Ona and my life as it was before. You know what happens? I begin to feel like I'm suffocating. It feels like I'm dying.

"Ro, you got to get some therapy. You've got a full-blown midlife crisis going on."

"Maybe."

"Ain't no maybe about it. Come on. Ona will kill me if I don't have you back on time. We can talk more in the car."

Chapter 33

Ona made her way up the park's gravel path. She could see the boys playing on the jungle gym, Solis watching them from the bench outside the play area.

She wasn't sure if she was doing the right thing. Was it her imagination? The loving glances, the body language . . . Could she be reading too much into it? She'd let suspicion get the better of her before; she couldn't afford to do it again.

"Hey, Ona, I wasn't expecting you. I thought you had to work late." Solis greeted Ona, as she came up.

"I hope getting the boys wasn't a problem." Ona replied.

"Not at all. The boys and I were going to catch a movie after lunch. Care to join us?"

"Thank you, but no, I have to get back. I just stopped by because I wanted to talk with you."

"What about?"

Ona sat down on the bench next to Solis. "I don't know how to say this, but I need to ask. Has Ronin been inappropriate with you in any way?"

"Ona, I rarely see Mr. Jackson. I spend all my time with the boys. You know that."

"If Ronin touched you or made advances, it wouldn't be your fault. You can tell me."

"Ona, I have no idea what you are talking about."

"Something isn't right."

"Ona, if you feel that way, maybe I shouldn't take care of the boys anymore."

"Solis, I didn't mean—I'd hate for you to quit. The boys love you."

"I'll miss them; but I'm sure you can find someone else."

"Solis, we should talk about this."

"I'm sorry, Ona, I have to go."

"Solis, you're upset. Did something happen?"

Solis left before Ona could say any more. Stunned, Ona watched Solis run for the bus. It was obvious she was crying. The conversation hadn't gone the way she expected. But, then what did she expect? She'd accused the girl of sleeping with her husband. Quitting and running away in tears would be a reasonable reaction.

Her phone rang. It was Joi. She'd snuck out of the office without telling anyone.

"Where are you? We have a conference in an hour." Joi asked.

"At the park. I'll be late getting back to the office. I have to take the boys to lunch and then see if Audra can come get them."

"What's wrong? What happened?"

"Everything is wrong. I asked Solis if she was sleeping with Ronin," Ona answered solemnly.

"I can't believe it. When? I wasn't sure you'd do it. What'd she say?"

"Just now. She denied it and quit on the spot. I should never have asked her. It was stupid."

"She's lying," Joi said flatly.

"She could be telling the truth. The boys really love Solis."

"The boys will get over it. You needed to get that girl out of your house."

"Joi, I'm accusing him of having an affair with an underage girl. Do you know what that means?"

"Did you see the looks between them? I did. You ever heard of hiding in plain sight? Find a new sitter."

"What if I'm wrong? What if he finds out I talked to Solis?"

"I wouldn't say anything to Ronin unless he asks. If he does, tell him she can't do it anymore because of school or some shit."

"Joi, I love him. I won't put my kids through a divorce."

"Ona, he may not give you a choice."

"Mommy!" Robert ran over, arms outstretched.

"Joi, I have to go." Ona hung up; and caught Robert as he jumped into her arms. "Hey, love bug."

Ronin Jr. made his way over more slowly. He looked around. "Where's Solis?" he asked.

"She had to go. So, we are going to lunch and then to see Nana." Ona answered.

"Is she okay? She didn't say goodbye. She always says goodbye."

"I'm sure she wanted to, but she was in a hurry. Come on, let's go."

Ona tried to sound upbeat. His sadness broke her heart. How was she going to explain that there would be no more goodbyes, no more Solis?

*****

Iris sat on the floor next to Solis. "Solis talk to me. What happened? Do I need to call Marlon?"

Solis lay on the floor, tears streaming down her face. "She knows. It's over."

"Shit! How do you know?

"She asked me. She came to the park. I was with the boys."

"What'd you say?"

"I lied, and I quit."

"Quit? Does he know?"

"No. I don't want . . . I love him. I just can't. What am I going to do, Iris?"

"I'm sorry, Solis. I don't know."

Dahlia knocked on Solis' bedroom door, cracking it slightly. "Hi, Iris."

"Hello, Ms. Dahlia," Iris replied.

"Solis, you're not babysitting tonight?" Dahlia asked, curious.

Solis wiped her face; quickly regaining her composure. "Mrs. Jackson changed her work schedule to spend more time with the boys. She doesn't need me for a while."

"Strange. Women like her don't want to spend time with their kids. That's why they hire nannies. Has Mr. Jackson been paying you any extra attention? You know, being around when Mrs. Jackson isn't?"

"Dahlia, Mr. Jackson isn't like that."

"Men will be men. Mrs. Jackson knows that."

"Oh my god, Dahlia, I spend all of my time with the boys. I rarely see him. The Jacksons are nice people. I love watching the boys."

"I just want to make sure you aren't giving him any more for his money. Men like him are used to getting what they want."

Solis grabbed a book from a shelf and hurled it at Dahlia. Dahlia moved just in time to avoid getting hit.

"I am no whore, you crazy bitch!" Solis screamed. "You're a sorry excuse for a mother. If I am fucking him, what are you going to do about it? Huh? What? Storm over there and demand he confess? Negotiate better rates for my services? Threaten to call the police? I'm warning you, Dahlia. If you hurt Ronin, I'll end you—end you! Get out!"

Solis slammed the door in Dahlia's face and locked it. Devastated, she dropped to the floor.

"Solis. What the hell!"

"I hate her! I hate them both! Ona . . . Dahlia . . . I hate them!" Solis sobbed.

"You should call Ronin."

"No! Calling him will only make things worse. He'll . . . you don't know him. If he finds out I'm hurt . . . he'll do something crazy. The boys? I didn't say goodbye to them. They'll be so hurt. Oh god! Iris . . ."

Dahlia stood outside Solis' room. She'd called him Ronin, not Mr. Jackson. Coupled with the money, the time, the attention, and the book to the face, it was clear—Solis was sleeping with him. She'd seen it before. She'd lived it. The question was, what was she going to do about it?

Chapter 34

Ronin hadn't seen or heard from Solis in two weeks. There was no explanation. No calls. No text. Nothing. She was just gone. Ona wasn't any help, and asking the boys was out of the question. Amour et Chocolat was his only option.

"Where is she?" Ronin asked.

Marlon stopped stocking the shelf in front of him. "She isn't here."

"Marlon, I know you know what's going on. You're her cousin. She tells you everything."

"Piper, man the counter. I'll be back in ten."

Marlon motioned for Ronin to go outside as he came around the counter. Once outside, Marlon turned to him.

"You need to go back to your wife."

"What? Marlon, tell me what the hell is going on. I'm worried about her. She won't answer my calls."

"Trust me, she's doing you a favor."

"Marlon, I'm asking you to talk to me."

Ronin's patience was running thin. If he didn't get what he wanted from Marlon, he was going to find her one way or another.

"Do you love Solis enough to leave her alone?"

"If that's what she wants, she'll have to tell me that herself."

"You're willing to risk your whole life to be with her?"

"Yes."

"Don't you think Solis knows that? Did it ever occur to you that she isn't willing to let you do that?"

"That isn't up to her."

"Not up to her?"

"Marlon, enough. Where can I find Solis?"

"You want to know what's going on? Ask your wife. She came to the park a couple of weeks ago and asked Solis if she was sleeping with you. Solis told her she wasn't and quit. It gets worse. Dahlia suggested all the gifts and money you gave her were payment for other services rendered."

"Why didn't she tell me? What kind of mother does that shit? Is Solis okay? I got to talk to her. Where is she?"

"She figured it'd be better if she just left you alone. She didn't want to mess things up for you."

"Where is she?"

"At home. I'll tell her you came by." Marlon went back inside.

Ronin was enraged. He'd felt Ona's suspicions growing over the past few weeks, but he never dreamed in a million years, she would talk to Solis. Asking him was one thing. Going behind his back and asking Solis was another. And Ona knew it.

*****

After the blowout with Dahlia and the breakup, Solis was in no condition to deal with anyone, least of all a lovesick boyfriend. But Ronin wasn't going anywhere. Annoyed, Marlon called Solis.

"Solis?"

"Hey, cuz. What's up? If you need me to, I'll come in."

"No. That's not why I called. Girl, Ronin was just here. You need to talk to the brother. Ignoring him isn't going to work. He clearly hasn't taken the hint."

"What? What'd you tell him?"

"I told him everything. He said he'd only leave you alone if you asked him to. I think he's going to come clean. I got to get back. I call you later."

"Marlon, wait—"

He was gone. It only took a minute for the phone to ring. It was Ronin. Against her better judgement; she answered.

"Ronin, why can't you leave well enough alone? I gave you an out. Ona believes me. Dahlia believes me. You could just go on with your life. Why? Why are you making this so hard?" Solis sobbed.

"I want to talk to you," Ronin pleaded.

"Why? What's there to say? No. It hurts bad enough. You're only making it worse." Solis hung up.

"Goddamn stubborn woman!" Ronin shouted.

He knew calling her again would be pointless. She would just ignore the call and send him to voice mail like she'd done for weeks. Solis was trying to protect him. She had given him the perfect out. He wasn't going to take it.

Ronin started the car. He had two destinations: The first was to take the boys to his parents. The second, was to deal with Ona.

*****

Ona wasn't home when he got there. The house was empty, as if the family that lived there had vanished, leaving all the trappings of their lives behind. A myriad of emotions assailed him, guilt being the most salient. But what wasn't there was a desire to change course. He was resolute. It was over.

Ona opened the front door. "Ronin?"

"I'm in the kitchen." He called back.

Ona put her bags down in the foyer. "Mmm . . . smells good. When did you learn to cook?"

"I didn't. I'm just good at faking it. Take out from Peking. Have some wine."

"Where are the boys?"

"With Byron and Audra. We need to talk."

"About?"

"About you asking Solis if I was sleeping with her."

"Ronin, you have to understand, I got the feeling . . . you've been distracted lately, and then there were little things. I didn't think at first . . . she's so young, you wouldn't . . ."

"And you decided to confront Solis instead of just asking me?"

"I should've asked you. I was just afraid—"

"Afraid I'd lie? Or afraid I'd tell the truth?"

"Ronin don't be ridiculous. I get why you're mad, but she quit, and it's over. Maybe it's for the best. The boys were getting too attached, don't you think?"

"Ona, I'm sleeping with Solis."

Ona threw the wine in his face. "You son of a bitch! Sleeping with her? As in more than once? How long have you been with her?"

Ronin wiped his face with a napkin. "Since Mexico."

"Ronin, are you crazy? She's a teenager for Christ's sake!" Ona shrieked.

"I know better than anyone who and what Solis is."

"Ronin, why? Why?" Ona cried.

"I don't know why. I can't explain it. I'm not even going to try."

"Not even going to try—do you even care what happens to you? Happens to us? The boys?"

"I care."

"Then leave her," Ona demanded.

"Leave me," Ronin answered back.

"You'd throw all this away?" Ona said, raising her arms. "Ten years for what? Her? She's still in high school. The girl isn't even old enough to drink!"

"This isn't about her. It's about us."

"Not about her? It's all about her. What'd she do? Seduce you?"

"I seduced her."

"I'll bet you aren't the first."

Ronin's face went cold. "I am the first. I am the only."

"How do you know? She's a fantastic liar! I know. I believed her."

"I'd show you the blood-stained sheets, but I left them in México."

Ona struck Ronin's face with such force the hit echoed in the empty house.

"Don't ever say that to me again. Not ever. Who are you? It's like I don't even know you. You took the girl's virginity and sent her back to the hotel room? So, you could what? Drown your guilt in a bottle? Oh my god, Ronin!"

"This conversation is over."

Ronin got up from the table. Ona followed him.

"Ronin, where are you going? We need to talk about this. I'm not going to let our marriage fall apart over some teenage girl you're infatuated with. You clearly aren't thinking straight."

"My parents will bring the boys home Monday. I'll call you."

Ronin grabbed his bag and left.

Chapter 35

Ronin waited by the gate, just outside the gym. It was a risk, coming to Solis's school, but he didn't know any other way to find her. He'd spent the night adrift on a turbulent sea of desire and desperation, Solis calling to him like a siren from the shore. In the light of day, he'd found himself shipwrecked; his life and possibly his freedom lost to the sea.

Solis and a group of cheerleaders filed out of the gym. Ronin held back, not wanting to be seen. He could tell Solis wasn't herself; her body carried a sadness, unnatural to her. Solis was as tough as she was fragile. Until he talked to her, he wouldn't know what damage Ona and Dahlia had done.

"Ronin!" Solis ran toward him, crying.

"I'm here. Solis, why didn't you come to me? Why didn't you tell me what was going on?"

"I couldn't. I knew you would do something stupid like leave Ona. I didn't want that."

"You don't need to worry about Ona. She is for me to deal with. Or Dahlia. I know what she said to you. You are not my whore. I do what I do for you because I love you. If Dahlia was anyone other than your mother . . ."

"Ronin, you shouldn't be here."

"Marlon said you wanted me to leave you alone. Is that what you want?"

"I don't want to leave you. I love you, Ronin. But now that Ona knows . . ."

"Solis, I love you. Nothing will keep me from you. Nothing."

"I don't want to go home. I want to stay with you."

"Dahlia?"

"I don't care about Dahlia. I'll call Marlon. If he knows where I am, it should be fine."

"Okay. Let's go."

*****

Dahlia tapped on Solis' bedroom door. She didn't answer. She tried the doorknob; it wasn't locked.

"Solis. Are you . . .?" Dahlia sighed. Solis wasn't there.

Dahlia peeked her head in Marlon's room. "Where's Solis?"

"Damn, Dahlia, do you knock?"

"It's after midnight. Solis never stays out this late. If she isn't at work or cheer, she's here."

"Why are you asking me?"

"She isn't talking to me. I know she'd never go anywhere without telling you."

"You called her a whore. And you wonder why she isn't here? You got to be kidding me."

"I didn't mean it the way she took it. I just wanted to—"

"Didn't mean it? You said she was so lovable she made you sick. Or were you too drunk to remember that?"

"I may be a bad mother, but I'm still her mother."

"If you were her mother, you'd know where she is. If you were her mother, you wouldn't have said those things."

"I messed up. Are you going to keep beating me over the head or tell me where she is?"

"Why do you care, Dahlia? Really?"

"I just want to know if she's okay."

"You want to know if she's with him."

"Is she?"

Marlon loved Dahlia. She and Solis were his only family. They loved him unconditionally. He wanted to protect them both, Solis from

Dahlia and Dahlia from herself. It was a tight rope to walk. Dahlia's concern seemed genuine, but genuine or not, he had no intention of breaking Solis' confidence. He knew she was safe. That would have to be enough for Dahlia. To be fair, he would call Solis and tell her to come home tomorrow.

"Solis is okay. I'll make sure she's home tomorrow. If you want to know where she was, you can ask her yourself . . . tomorrow."

"I know she's with him. He's too old for her Marlon, and you know it."

"It doesn't matter. Solis will be eighteen in December. Let it go."

"Tell me where she is. I'll call the police and send them to his house. I'm sure his wife would appreciate that."

"Call them. Go search for her. Turn me in for not telling you where she is. Turn him in for sleeping with her. Do all of it. It's your right. I applaud your newfound desire to be a better mother, but you can't do it overnight. I know Solis, and I'm telling you the best way to handle this is to wait until she comes home tomorrow and talk to her. Good night."

Chapter 36

Solis shivered as he ran his hands down the length of her body. Desire wanted to wake her. Reason decided to let her sleep. They'd made love until the wee hours of the morning. Solis pushed the limits of his emotional and physical stamina. She was reckless, untamed. The knowledge that he was the only one to have her this way stirred feelings of possession in the basest parts of him.

A year ago, he was a reasonably happy married man with two wonderful kids. Today he was a man desperately in love with a woman less than half his age. A man who had left his wife, turned his kids' lives upside down, and put his ability to practice law in jeopardy. He was digging his own grave and pulling the dirt down on top of him. The problem was he couldn't stop digging. Lost in thought, the ringing of the bedside phone startled him.

"I didn't ask for a wakeup call," Ronin answered.

"Get your ass down here." Byron demanded.

"Dad?"

"Is she with you?"

"Who?"

"Don't play dumb with me, Ronin. Get down here. Meet me in the bar."

"How the hell did you know where I was?"

"You aren't the first man to have a mistress. In the bar. Five minutes." Byron hung up.

*****

Byron sat at the bar. How the hell was he going to convince his son to go back to Ona and the boys? He had a strong suspicion Ronin was in love with Solis. If that was true, convincing him to return home would be difficult, if not impossible.

"Dad, what are you doing here?"

"You're asking me that question? What are you doing here? Better yet, what are you doing here with a sixteen-year-old girl in your hotel room?"

"Solis is seventeen."

"Sixteen, seventeen, who gives a shit? Ronin, are you willing to throw your whole life away for this girl? Don't get me wrong, she's beautiful, and I'm sure she's a great time, but you got to end it."

"Solis is not a great time. If you ever refer to Solis as a 'great time' again, this conversation is over."

"You're in love with her."

"Yes, I am. God help me, I am. I can't be without her. I've tried. Hell, she left me—left me for my own good. You know what I did? I did everything in my power to find her and bring her back to me. If she left me now, I'd do the same."

"I warned you. I told you it'd come to this. What did I say?"

"I know you did. You told me to leave her alone. I couldn't. I tried."

"What does she have on you? Is she pregnant? Threatened to tell Ona? Or her parents?"

"Solis doesn't have anything on me. She hasn't said a word to anyone about it. Her mother and Ona both confronted her. She said nothing. Solis doesn't want to take me away from Ona and the boys. She is content to be my mistress."

"Of course, she is. You tell her you love her, and she knows you mean it. You shower her with gifts. You're older and more experienced, so the sex is good. She isn't old enough to have had enough men to think otherwise. For a young girl, that is enough."

"You don't know Solis. There haven't been any other men."

"Boy, calm down. Solis is young, beautiful, and from the sound of it, damn smart. I know you well enough to know that she'd have to be. Did you ever stop to think that you may not be good for Solis? What about her parents? I'm sure they wouldn't appreciate the fact that you've deflowered their daughter and are keeping her as a mistress."

"Her father is doing life for murder. Her mother, I don't know."

"When does she turn eighteen? Soon, I hope. At seventeen, you're in a bit of a legal gray area. I doubt you'd be charged with a felony, but even a misdemeanor can carry jail time. You could lose your ability to practice law."

"She turns eighteen in December."

"You're really in love with her, aren't you?"

"Yes."

"I can't stop you from keeping her as a mistress, but you have to go home to your wife and kids. You must take care of home first. Understand?"

"I understand."

"I think it'd be better if the boys stayed with your mother and me for a while. You and Ona have a lot of things to work out. The boys don't need to be there for that. Take a few more days. Get your shit together and go home."

*****

Solis didn't answer the first few times he called. Marlon was a more than a little upset when she finally did.

"Solis!"

"What?" Solis snapped back, barely awake.

"Dahlia is tripping. You need to come home."

"Let her trip, Marlon. I don't care."

"Listen to me, bring your ass home. Today. If you don't, I'll come get you. To keep Dahlia from putting an APB out on you last night, I promised I'd make sure you were home today. Got it?"

"Fine. I'll have Ronin drop me off as soon as I can."

"Before five, Solis. Not a minute after. Dahlia will be home at six."

"Damn, Marlon, don't get your panties in a bunch, I'll be there."

Solis ended the call. She was about to call Ronin's cell when he returned.

"Hello, lover. Where you been? I clearly didn't do my job if you felt like leaving the bed this morning." Solis smiled.

"If you did anymore, I'd be incapacitated. I'm sorry I had to leave. Byron came looking for me."

"Your dad? What are you sixteen?" Solis laughed.

"Apparently, I haven't been making the best decisions of late." Ronin grinned.

"That makes two of us. Marlon called while you were gone. I need you to drop me off before five. Dahlia gets off at six. It seems she's caught a sudden case of motherhood."

"Not a problem. I need to check in on the boys. I haven't seen them since Friday."

"Just the boys? What about Ona?"

"Solis, I'm not going back to Ona. I'm going to file for divorce."

"No. If she'll take you back, go back."

"You want me to stay with her?"

"I don't want the boys to grow up without their father or, worse, blame me for breaking up your marriage. I grew up without a father and with a bitter angry mother. That's exactly what Ona will be. You can't do that to them."

"I'll always be a father to my boys. You didn't break up my marriage. I'm leaving Ona because I'm not in love with her anymore. She deserves better."

"Ronin, I don't want you to feel like you have to do this for me. I'm fine. I love you. I'm happy."

"Solis Monroe, you may be content to be my mistress, but I'm not content for you to be. You may be okay with it now, but that won't always be the case. I know you."

"True. I'm afraid you'll make this decision and regret it. Maybe even regret me. You've been married to Ona for ten years. That's a long time. We've only been together a little more than a year."

"I will never regret you. I love you. I need you to believe that. Do you?"

"Yes. I know you love me. But I still want you to go back. Please. Ronin and Robert need you."

"What makes you think she'll take me back after this?"

"Who do you think sent Byron here? Ona is too insecure to let you divorce her. She wants you back. Go back."

"I want you."

"You have me. Matter of fact, you can have me right now."

"Not if you want to get home by five. If I don't get you out of here soon, I may never let you leave."

"Hang out the Do Not Disturb sign. We can kill an hour or two. It's only noon."

"Vile temptress."

"Oh, you poor man. I haven't even begun to tempt you."

*****

Dahlia was already home when Ronin dropped Solis off. She'd come home early to make sure Solis showed up.

"You were with him last night," Dahlia stated flatly.

"Is that a question or an accusation?" Solis replied.

"Solis, he is too old for you. Not to mention, he's married."

"I don't care."

"I could call the police. I should call the police. I should call his wife."

"And say what? I'll just deny it. You can't prove anything. As for his wife, she already knows."

"I know you're old for your age. You always have been. I can understand why you'd be attracted to Ronin and why he'd be attracted to you. It just can't be."

"Why? I'm not trying to marry him. We enjoy each other's company. I still have a lot of things to do in my life."

"What kind of mother would I be if I let you do this?"

"The kind of mother you've always been. How are you going to stop me, Dahlia? Are you going to ground me? Send me to my room? What?"

Dahlia slapped Solis across the face. Solis' rubbed her cheek; a murderous look in her eye. Freighted, Dahlia stepped back.

"I'm sorry Solis. I just—,"

"You what? Want to play mom? It's too late for that, Dahlia. Don't you see that? We've never been mother and daughter—ever. You can't go back. I know you regret having me. You resent me with every breath you take."

"Solis, I do love you. I do. I know I haven't been the best mom, and there is no excuse for that. I just know that this is going to end badly. That woman isn't going to stand by and let you take her husband."

"I'm not taking her husband. He's leaving her."

"She won't see it that way. If I were her, I wouldn't see it that way."

"Dahlia, I'm not going to stop seeing him. I love him."

Dahlia could see she wasn't getting anywhere. Solis was too stubborn to listen. She was in love with Ronin. Dahlia didn't doubt he was in love with her. She'd never met a man who didn't love Solis. Keeping Solis away from Ronin would be an impossible task.

"Solis, what can I do to make you see how wrong this is?"

"Nothing. Ronin is off-limits."

"Solis, you can't seriously think I can agree to that."

"Those are my terms. Take them or leave them."

"You may be five months shy of eighteen, but you're in my house, and I dictate the terms here."

"You want me to leave?"

Dahlia's heart stopped. She had seen this all before. Only this time she was the mother and Solis was the child. Solis wasn't going to stay with the parents of some guy who knocked her up. Judging by the way

Ronin lavished gifts and money on her, he would probably put her up in an apartment all her own. Dahlia steadied her nerves. She knew whatever she said next would make or break their relationship, possibly forever.

"I don't want you to leave, but we have to deal with this. I'm trying to protect you."

"Dahlia, I don't know what to say. I love him. I know he's married. I know he's forty. None of that matters to me. I wish it didn't matter to the rest of the world. I'm not naïve enough to think it wouldn't. I can't do what you are asking me to do. I just can't."

Solis went to her room and closed the door.

Chapter 37

"He hasn't come home yet?" Joi asked.

"No, it's been two weeks," Ona responded tearfully.

"Where are the boys? With Audra?"

"Yes. Byron and Audra thought it best that the boys stay with them while Ronin and I worked things out. If we work things out. I agreed. Byron said he talked to Ronin and tried to get him to see reason. He isn't home yet . . . so I don't know."

"It's time to confront him. Tell him to leave her. He can't be stupid enough to leave you and the boys for some teenager."

"Joi, the last time I confronted Ronin, he left. Next time, he may leave and never come back. I don't know, Joi. I think he is in love with her."

"In love with her? Please. He's in love with what's between her legs."

"I know Ronin. It isn't all about the sex. She managed to seduce my husband in my house right under my nose."

"Ona, you have to decide. If Ronin is dumb enough to leave his family for a seventeen-year-old girl, then you're better off. If you really want to fight for your marriage, then you got to get rid of her once and for all. Confront her. Put the little bitch in her place. Tell her to stay away from your husband. Where does she work? You said he met her in the mall, right? I say you take a shopping trip."

"You're right. I'll swing by tomorrow. Maybe I can catch her when she gets off. After I set her straight, I'll talk to Ronin."

"Good. If that doesn't work, you could always kill him." Joi laughed.

*****

"Welcome to the Amour et Chocolat. Can I help you . . . Ona, what are you doing here?"

"As a matter of fact, you can. You can stay the hell away from my husband."

"Ona, this is not the time or the place for this conversation. You really should be talking to Ronin. Not me."

"You can't have him. What? Do you think you can replace me? Do you think you can take my life? Did you think I'd let you sleep in my bed? Stay in my house? Raise my children?"

Ona was loud and attracting the attention of the other patrons. Solis tried to manage the situation.

"Ona, you're angry, and you've every right to be. You should really talk to Ronin about this."

"Talk to him? You know, he hasn't been home in two weeks! Do you think I'm a fool? He thinks he is in love with you!"

"Ona, you should go. I have work to do and customers waiting."

"I'm not going anywhere until you tell me that you're leaving my husband."

"Ona, you need to leave."

"You're a fucking whore!"

Ona was shouting. Piper ran to the back to find Marlon. He told her to call mall security and quickly left the storeroom for the lobby. Ona was standing in the middle of the store screaming at the top of her lungs. The other shoppers looked on, unsure of what to do.

"Whore! Bitch! You can't have him. I won't let you. Do you hear me, bitch? Stay the hell away from my husband."

Marlon stepped out from behind the counter. "Solis, go to the back and stay there."

Solis was slipping off her apron when mall security arrived.

The guard spoke calmly. "Ma'am, you're going to need to leave. Please follow us out of the store. We'll escort you from the mall." He reached for Ona's arm.

"Don't touch me! I don't need you to escort me anywhere." Ona shouted, pulling away.

"Ma'am, if you make me ask you again, I will call the police."

"I'm leaving." Ona stormed out, the security guard following closely behind.

Solis took a deep breath. All eyes in the store were on her.

"Ladies and gentlemen, I apologize for the scene you just witnessed. I assure you all is well. Please have a sample on the house, and we'll be with each one of you in a moment."

"Solis, are you okay? You sure you don't want to go? Maybe talk to a certain someone?" Marlon asked, worried.

"I am fine, Marlon."

Solis stepped to the counter and began to assist customers as if nothing had happened. She overheard two ladies talking about the scene Ona made.

"I don't know if I could be that calm if some woman came to my job acting a fool and accusing me of sleeping with her husband. She's a better woman than me."

"Have you ever seen anything more pathetic? I'll be damned if I make a scene like that over any man. Husband or not. What'd she think the girl was going to do?"

"I don't know. What I do know is that the brother is going to have hell to pay when he gets home."

"When he gets home? You mean, if he comes home."

The women laughed together as they approached the counter.

Solis greeted them. "Will this be all, ladies?"

"I'd like one of those samples."

"Try this one. It is called Simply Sinful. It's one of our best truffles," Solis offered.

"This is good." The woman turned to her friend. "Try it."

Solis handed one to her friend. "That will be forty-five dollars."

The older woman paid while her friend busily ate her sample.

"Thank you. Please come again."

Solis stepped back from the counter. The calm façade she wore during Ona's verbal assault was fading. Ona's emotional outburst changed things. The last time Ona confronted her, she left. Solis had no intention of leaving this time.

"Marlon, I'm going to take my lunch."

Chapter 38

It was nine fifteen. Solis sat in English Literature, barely able to hold her head up as waves of nausea assailed her. All week, she'd had flu like symptoms. She thought nothing of it until this morning.

The classroom phone rang.

"Solis, you are wanted in the office. Take your things," Mrs. Greiner instructed. "You will not be back before class is over."

Solis was too ill to inquire the reason for the call. She collected her things and left. Outside, she was met by the school counselor.

"Solis, are you feeling okay?" Mr. Hans asked, concerned.

"I'm fine."

"I wanted to talk with you before we head into the conference room. Your mother, a social worker from child welfare, and a police officer are here to speak with you. I didn't want you to walk into the meeting surprised."

Dahlia. Solis only half believed her when she left last night after their fight. Dahlia demanded she end things with Ronin—again. She refused—again. The argument became so heated Marlon had to separate them. Dahlia went to her room. Solis left to spend the night with Ronin.

Ronin wanted to take her home this morning; he didn't think she was well enough to be at school. Solis insisted he take her anyway. Now she wished she had listened to him.

"Solis, are you sure you're all right?" Mr. Hans asked, concerned.

"I am fine."

Solis could feel the vomit in the back of her throat. She held it back. She would need her wits about her if she was going to get out of this. She did not have time to be sick. She took a seat in the conference room next to who she guessed was the social worker. The officer was in uniform.

"Solis, are you okay? You don't look well," the woman asked.

"I'm fine. Who are you?"

"I'm Nancy Reynolds, a social worker from the county. I was asked here today by your mother and Officer Stanton."

"Why?" Solis asked flatly, fighting back an ever-worsening nausea.

"We have some concerns that you may be in an unsafe relationship," Nancy responded. "We'd like to know where you were last night."

She was with Ronin. Dahlia knew it. Solis figured it was safe to assume everyone else knew it too. She decided the best course of action was to be guarded.

"Why?" Solis asked again.

"Where were you?" Officer Stanton asked.

"Am I under arrest? Have I committed a crime, Officer Stanton?"

"No. We are just trying to gather information. Like Ms. Reynolds said, we are all concerned for your safety."

"I appreciate your concern. I can assure you I'm not in any danger."

"Your mother seems to disagree. She believes you are in a relationship with an older man—a Mr. Jackson. I understand you have been working part time as a nanny for the family."

Officer Stanton's tone was stern and authoritative. Solis could tell he was not in the mood for her evasive and vague answers.

"Yes, I was," Solis answered.

"You aren't any longer?"

"No, I'm not."

"Tell the truth, Solis. You are sleeping with Ronin Jackson and you were with him last night."

"Mr. Jackson is a good man. He's never been inappropriate with me in any way."

"Solis, we've spoken with Mrs. Jackson, and she seems to agree with your mother that something is going on with you and Mr. Jackson. We are just trying to make sure you are okay." Officer Stanton tried to be direct while still showing concern.

Ms. Reynolds reached for Solis' hand. "Can you tell us where you were last night? Your mother believes you were with Mr. Jackson. Is that true?"

Solis felt her skin grow warm with fury. She took a deep breath, trying to quell her overwhelming need to vomit.

"I have no intention of telling anyone where I was last night. I've already answered your question about Mr. Jackson. May I go?"

Officer Stanton moved in closer. "No. No, you may not. Your mother told us you're a very smart girl. If you're sleeping with Mr. Jackson, he is committing a crime. Are you lying to protect him? I find it hard to believe that both his wife and your mother would have the same concerns if there was nothing going on."

"Officer Stanton, that's because you don't know Dahlia and Ona like I do. Let me tell you."

"Solis, you wouldn't." Dahlia stared at Solis in horror.

"The only unsafe relationship I've ever been in is with my mother. All my life, I've had to take care of her and myself. She's clinically depressed and falls into catatonic states for days on end. She's a borderline alcoholic. I don't have enough fingers to count how many times I've come home to find her drunk. In all her concern, did she tell you she'd accused me of being Mr. Jackson's whore? Of course, she didn't because she's a liar."

"I'm not a liar!" Dahlia shouted. "That was then. This is now. I'm trying to protect you."

Officer Stanton held Dahlia back, forcing her into the seat. "Ms. Scott, I will have to ask you to sit down." Dahlia sat still.

Solis could see the pain in Dahlia's eyes but continued without hesitation.

"Mr. and Mrs. Jackson are having marital problems. Mrs. Jackson confronted me a few weeks ago, and I told her the same thing I told you. I quit that same day and haven't been back since. She came to my job and made a scene. You can ask mall security, I'm sure there's a record of it. Apparently, she's done that before to another woman. As the help, you hear things. Her marriage is falling apart. What better scapegoat than the nanny? Mr. Hans, may I go now?"

"Solis, Officer Stanton, Ms. Reynolds, and I appreciate your honesty. I know this is difficult."

"Hold on, Mr. Hans. Solis, I'm not convinced that there's nothing happening between you and Mr. Jackson. I'm going to question Mr. Jackson. I don't know where you were last night, but I do know where you will be tonight and every night from now on—at home. Are we clear?"

Solis couldn't hold it any longer. She ran to the nearest waste bin and vomited.

"From the looks of it, home is where you should be now." Officer Stanton helped Solis to her seat.

"I agree. I'll get her released. Ms. Scott, you can take her home. Officer, Ms. Reynolds, we can continue this conversation in my office. I have some concerns about this meeting."

Solis knew Mr. Hans well enough to know he was very unhappy with the way Officer Stanton had treated her. She was sure her comments about Dahlia, although not addressed, didn't go over well either. She didn't care.

"How could you?" Dahlia cried, shaking her head. "How could you? I'm your mother. Why did you tell them that? Why?"

Solis stood up slowly. "I warned you, Dahlia. I told you if you hurt Ronin, I'd end you. I meant it."

"We can't live together like this, Solis."

"No. No, we can't."

*****

Instead of getting better, the nausea and vomiting got worse. Solis was exhausted. Marlon insisted she go to the doctor. She made an appointment and called Iris for a ride.

The nurse at the clinic gave her an injection for the nausea, started her on IV fluids, and ordered labs. Solis was beginning to feel a lot better by the time she returned.

"Ms. Monroe, I can tell you for certain that you don't have the stomach flu—you're pregnant."

"Not possible. I'm on the pill. I take them every day like clockwork. This isn't supposed to happen. I don't believe you. I want you to run the test again. You must've gotten it confused with some other woman."

"I understand you're upset. Would you like me to get your friend from the waiting area? For a little support."

"Yes! Get Iris! Please."

Solis was frantic and on the verge of a total meltdown when the nurse returned with Iris.

"It's going to be okay, Solis," Iris tried to console her.

"No! No, it isn't."

"Solis, you have options," the nurse offered reassuringly.

"Options? You mean like an abortion? I took the pill. Why didn't it work? Nobody told me it wouldn't work!"

"No method of birth control is 100 percent effective. Pregnancy is always a risk."

"Oh my god. This can't be happening. Ronin is going to be so angry. He'll think I did it on purpose."

Iris held her hand. "Ronin loves you. He won't think that."

"It's a lot to take in. Do you know when you had your last period?"

"Oh my god! I don't remember. I always have them. I don't remember."

"Let's do an ultrasound to find out. That way, we can make a more informed decision."

The nurse put the probe on her belly. The room filled with the sound of the baby's heartbeat. Solis began to cry. It was really happening. She was pregnant.

"Solis . . ." Iris stared at the monitor in disbelief.

"Solis, you're about sixteen weeks. You haven't had a period for a while."

She didn't need the nurse to tell her that. The picture was worth a thousand words. There it was—a baby. Solis closed her eyes and wept.

Chapter 39

"Mr. Jackson, I appreciate you taking the time to meet with me." Officer Stanton took a seat in the chair across from Ronin's desk.

"No problem. What's this about?"

Ronin knew. Solis told him to expect a visit from Officer Stanton a week ago. He was more worried about Solis than the officer's visit. She sounded sick when they spoke over the phone. They'd agreed it would be best not to see each other for a while; a separation would give the situation a chance to cool down and give him time to settle things with Ona.

"I'm going to be frank. It's been brought to our attention that you may be involved in a sexual relationship with a minor. Her name is Solis Monroe."

"Did my wife or her mother send you? Maybe both? My wife thinks Solis is my mistress and her mother thinks she's my whore. She's neither."

"You knew I was coming. Did Solis tell you to expect me?" "With my wife, it was only a matter of time before the authorities made their way to my door. Solis stopped working for us abruptly. I wasn't sure why. I didn't think anything of it until I ran into her cousin Marlon, and he told me about my wife verbally attacking Solis at work and interrogating her in front of our children. If that wasn't bad enough, Solis' mother struck her and accused her of being my whore. Marlon asked me to get my wife under control and to stay away from Solis. I tried to talk to Solis, to apologize, but she wouldn't return my calls."

"That's a lot. Question, was Solis with you last Sunday evening?"

"Why do you ask?"

"Her mother seems to think she was. Was she?"

"Since I haven't spoken to her, I'd suggest you ask Solis about her whereabouts."

"You're saying she wasn't with you?"

"I'm saying if you want to know where Solis was, you should ask her."

"I did. Oddly, she wouldn't say."

"Sounds like she doesn't want you to know."

"It does, doesn't it. Where were you last Sunday night, Mr. Jackson?"

"My comings and goings are none of your concern. Is there anything else, Officer?"

"Mr. Jackson, I find you curious. When accused of doing anything inappropriate with a minor, most men are angry and immediately start proclaiming their innocence to anyone who will listen. If I asked any other man that question; they'd be falling all over themselves to prove their whereabouts. You, not so much."

"I'm an attorney. There's no need. If you had any evidence, I'd done something wrong, I'd be at the station."

"True. But that may change. I'd advise you to keep your distance, Mr. Jackson."

"Is that all, officer?" Ronin asked, trying to hide his irritation.

"For now. I'll see myself out."

Ronin watched him leave. It was a warning. Officer Stanton didn't believe him. He wasn't going anywhere.

"Ronin, Tasha said the police were here. What the hell is going on?" Damien asked.

"Calm down. Officer Stanton just left. Dahlia and Ona pulled the trigger."

"I told you this would happen. What'd you say? And why did you talk to him without me?"

"I didn't deny it. I didn't confess either. Without any evidence, there isn't much he can do. No charges are being filed. He just warned me off."

"Yet—no charges are being filed yet. What did Solis say?"

"She was masterful. As a defense attorney, you'd have been impressed."

"Impressed? It was more likely. He thought Solis had been coached and is covering for you. This shit is over. Done. Today. I don't even want to hear Solis's name cross your lips. I'm serious, Ronin."

"You won't."

Damien stormed out.

Ronin fell back in his chair. He would have to go back. Ona wasn't going divorce him without a nasty fight. She'd see him in jail first. Then there was Dahlia. Reluctantly, Ronin picked up the phone.

"Ona."

"Ronin. Can we talk? You could come by the house tonight. The boys are still with your parents."

Every night Ona would ask when he was coming home, and every night he would answer "I don't know" or "Maybe, we will see," but not tonight.

"Yes, I'll be home tonight. We have a lot to talk about."

"We do. Come home."

"I'll see you tonight."

Ronin dropped his head on the desk. Solis wouldn't be eighteen for another four months. He would have to hold it together until then.

*****

Ona sat across the table from Ronin. She wasn't naïve. Officer Stanton brought Ronin home, not a desire to be with her. Ronin was saying all the things she wanted to hear but not what she wanted to know.

"Ona, I know I've hurt you. I'm not asking for forgiveness; I don't deserve it."

"Why, Ronin? I want to know why." Ona asked, upset.

"I can't answer that, Ona"

"That isn't good enough. If this is going to work. . . be honest with me. Why? Why her? She's a child, Ronin! A child! Is this some midlife crisis? Did you need to feel young again, more like a man? What?"

"Solis is not a child. And no. I don't need a woman to make me feel like a man. I need a woman who treats me like one."

"Like a man? What'd she do? Sex on command . . . whatever pleases you?"

"Solis is not my whore. Do you understand me?"

Ona sat back in her chair. "You love her."

"This isn't about Solis."

"Not about her? Then what's it about, Ronin?"

"You! You, Ona!" Ronin shouted.

"Me! You fucking the teenage nanny is my fault?" Ona yelled back.

"No, yes. I chose to cheat. That's mine. You . . . your insecurities and need to control everything is exhausting. The difference between you and Solis? No matter how much time and attention I give you, it's never enough. No matter how many times I tell you I love you or show you I love you, it doesn't change anything. You're angry and paranoid."

"I can't believe what I'm hearing. How dare you compare me with her? She's a teenager!"

"You wanted the truth, that is the truth."

"Insecure? Needy? Controlling? Angry? That's how you see me?"

"Why did you barge into my office? You humiliated me. Why? Because you thought I was cheating? You could've asked me, but you didn't. You asked Solis about our relationship behind my back too. You went to Solis' job."

"You were sleeping with Solis. That's different. And you know it!"

"Is it? What if I wasn't? What if you were wrong? Again, no trust. No respect. You call me incessantly to 'checkup' on me. I can't leave your side for more than hour without a text or a phone call. And it was like that before Solis."

"Don't turn this on me! You brought Solis into our home! Into our bed! You let our sons fall in love with her! Nothing I did . . . nothing I did is worse than that! Nothing!"

"You're right. So why do you want to stay with me? I seduced our teenage nanny and have carried on an affair with her for over a year. Why on earth would you still want me after that? Even if I promised to end it?"

"I want our family to stay together. The boys need their father. I'm not willing to let you throw away ten years of marriage over some teenage girl."

"I don't want to hurt you any more than I have. I want our family too, but I don't see how we move on from this. Do you? You're never going to forget this, even if you manage to forgive me."

"End it. Promise you'll never see her again. Go to counseling with me. Give us—give our family—a chance."

"Ona . . ."

"Promise me, Ronin."

"I won't see her again. I'll sleep in the guest room tonight."

Ona watched Ronin walk up the stairs. He was home. But Solis was still with him. She could feel it.

Chapter 40

Solis' head was spinning. She ran past Tasha's desk, just making it to the restroom.

"Solis?" Ronin jumped from behind his desk. The sound of Solis retching made his heart stop. A father of two, he knew the sound of morning sickness when he heard it.

"Solis, let me in."

"No. Go away."

Ronin hit the door with his shoulder. Solis was lying on the floor, sick, her skin ashen.

"Why didn't you tell me?" Ronin's voice was a mix of anger, shock, and concern.

"I knew you'd be upset, and I didn't want you to think I did it on purpose to trap you. I took my pills. I took them religiously. I don't know how this happened. The nurse said some shit about nothing being 100 percent."

"I know you well enough to know better than to think you'd try and trap me. I'm a grown man. I know how babies get made, and I know nothing is 100 percent. It's too late to care about that now. When did you find out?"

"Three weeks ago."

"Three weeks? And you're just telling me this now? How far along are you?"

Solis started to cry. Ronin knelt on the floor next to her. He could tell she was exhausted.

"How long have you been sick like this?"

"A month. I had to get IV fluids for dehydration at my first appointment. It's hard to take the anti-nausea pills. They make me sleepy, and I'm already beat. I can't eat anything. Everything comes back up."

"Dehydration? Solis, you're sick. Why in the hell are you at school, work, or anywhere? You should be in bed. You've been this sick and no one noticed?"

"Initially, I told them I had a bad case of the stomach flu. I use school as an excuse to work less. You know Dahlia is never home. I just stay in my room with ginger ale, crackers, and the medicine. I have a trash can in there."

"Solis!" Ronin shouted. The thought of her hiding in her room with crackers and a trash can made him furious.

"What'd you expect me to do? I can't tell anyone!" Solis shouted back.

"You could've told me. You should've told me. This is my fault. You can't have this baby."

"Stop it. You always do that. Why do you always do that? You didn't put me in this situation. We did. One minute, I'm your equal, and the next, I'm not. Treat me like your equal or leave me."

"Solis, you're seventeen. You have your whole life ahead of you."

"I want to have this baby. I don't have any other choice."

"Why do you think that? How far along are you? You never answered my question."

Solis lowered her head. Silent tears began to fall. "Five months."

"Solis, are you telling me you are five months pregnant? Are you sure?"

Solis lifted her sweater. There it was—a baby bump. He couldn't believe it. If she'd found out three weeks ago, she had to be four months along then. How on earth had he missed this?

"Ronin, please forgive me. I should've told you as soon as I found out. I was afraid. The nurse said I was too far along for an abortion. I didn't know. I swear it. I didn't know." Solis was trembling.

"There's nothing to forgive. I love you. Tell Dahlia. I'll deal with the consequences."

"No!" Solis pushed away from him.

"If you don't, I will."

"No. After the school meeting, I know what she'll do to you. You in jail or losing your job helps no one. Who's going to take care of us? The boys? Ona will take you to the cleaners in the divorce. She may take the boys from you. I'll be eighteen about the time the baby comes. I'll keep it from Dahlia if I can. When it becomes obvious, I won't tell anyone the baby is yours. We'll have to keep our distance until then. It has to be this way, and you know it."

"Fuck!" Ronin banged the back of his head against the door in frustration. The whole situation was surreal. Solis was going to ruin her whole life to keep him from going to jail.

"Tell Dahlia and Marlon today."

"No. I won't do it. I can take care of myself." Solis fell into Ronin exhausted.

Solis was obstinate. The fact that she was sick and afraid only made her more so. He could handle Dahlia and Ona. Solis was another matter entirely.

"Fine. I'll tell them myself."

"Ronin, please don't. Please," Solis begged in tears.

"Solis Monroe, listen to me. You are not going to be able to hide this pregnancy. You're ill, and someone needs to take care of you. You're in no condition to take care of yourself. I have a lot of things I need to do, namely divorce Ona before she gets wind of this, take care of the boys, get you prenatal care, figure out where you're going to live and how you're going to finish school. In order to do these things, I need to know you are safe and being well cared for. Today. Tell them today. If you don't call me tonight, I will be at your house in the morning."

"I am not a child! Stop treating me like one!"

"You aren't a child. You are a hardheaded woman who won't see reason. I know you are used to taking care of yourself, but that time is over now. It's my job to take care of you."

"Ronin, I'm scared. I'm tired."

Ronin could see the fear in her eyes. It broke him. "I know. I love you. We'll get through this. I'm going to take care of you. I promise. Say you believe me."

"I believe you. I love you."

"I love you too. Let's get you home and in bed."

Chapter 41

"Marlon." Solis' voice was faint.

Dahlia heard Solis' quiet cries and immediately knew something was wrong.

"Solis, are you okay?" Dahlia opened her bedroom door. "Marlon! Marlon! Marlon, get in here!" Dahlia screamed.

Marlon came through the door. Solis was on the floor next to a trash can with what appeared to be bile on her shirt. Her skin translucent.

"Dahlia call 911! Now! Go!"

Dahlia ran to get the phone. Marlon carried a lifeless Solis to the living room and laid her on the couch.

"It doesn't look like she's breathing! Oh god! She isn't breathing!" Dahlia shrieked.

Marlon could hear the 911 operator on the phone. He grabbed it from Dahlia. "She is breathing," Marlon reported to the operator.

"Check her pulse. Can you check it?" the operator asked.

Marlon placed his hand on Solis' wrist. "It is weak. Her breathing is shallow."

"Marlon don't let her die! Please!" Dahlia cried.

"Dahlia calm down! I can't hear!" Marlon shouted at her. "What now?"

"If she's vomiting, lay her on her side," the operator instructed him.

Marlon rolled Solis on to her side.

"My baby," Solis mumbled.

"Baby? What baby? Marlon, what is she talking about?" Dahlia asked, confused.

"Is she pregnant?" the operator asked, overhearing Dahlia's question.

Marlon lifted Solis' shirt. "She's pregnant."

"How far along is she? Roll her on her left side."

"I don't know," Marlon answered, rolling Solis on her side.

"Where are they? Why aren't they here yet?" Dahlia yelled angrily.

"The paramedics are three minutes out," the operator tried to reassure them. "How is she? Is she conscious?"

"No, ma'am, not anymore. Please hurry," Marlon pleaded. "Baby girl, why didn't you tell me? Why?"

The sound of sirens in the distance moved Dahlia into action. She ran outside to flag them down. Within minutes, EMS was putting Solis in the ambulance.

"We're taking her to Lake Methodist. There's no room in the ambulance. You'll have to follow." The paramedic closed the ambulance doors.

Dahlia and Marlon got in the car. Dahlia backed down the driveway at breakneck speed.

"Pregnant? Marlon, how did we miss that?"

"Easy—we weren't paying attention, and Solis didn't want us to know."

"Marlon, what if she—"

"Dahlia, that isn't going to happen."

*****

"We're looking for Solis Monroe. She was brought in by ambulance," Dahlia asked the first nurse she saw.

Before the nurse could answer, a doctor came through the emergency room doors. "You are her mother?" he asked.

"Yes," Dahlia responded.

"I am Dr. Lachlan, Solis treating physician. Solis is stable, but she isn't conscious. I have some questions. How long has she been like this?

When is the last time she was able to hold fluids down? Has she urinated in the last six hours?"

Dahlia stared at him unable to answer. Marlon stepped in.

"We don't know. I can guess she has been like this for at least the last eight hours. I haven't seen her since this morning. We found her like this forty-five minutes ago."

"Do you know if she has had any prenatal care?"

"I don't. I know she saw a doctor about a month ago. I thought she had the stomach flu."

"Are you the baby's father?"

"I'm her cousin. She lives with me and her mom."

"Is there anything else you can tell me about her?

"Nothing. She's always been healthy."

"I'm going to admit her. We're moving her to the OB floor. I've been an emergency room doctor for a long time, and I can honestly say I have treated marathon runners who weren't as dehydrated as she is. Why did you all wait so long to bring her in?"

"We didn't. I didn't know she was pregnant until today." Marlon replied. He could tell that wasn't the answer the doctor was looking for.

"Until today? Solis is five months pregnant. I'm not sure why she would go to such lengths to hide this pregnancy. If she had gone any longer, things could have been much worse. She is going to need a lot of rest and a lot more attention."

"Can we see her?" Dahlia asked.

"One at a time. When she is moved to the OB floor, she can have more visitors. I'll send the nurse out to get you in a moment." The doctor walked back through the emergency doors.

"I'm going to kill him. I'm going to kill him, Marlon. He's done. I'm calling Officer Stanton." Dahlia pulled her phone from her purse.

Marlon took the phone from Dahlia's hand. "Dahlia listen to me. This my fault. I knew about Ronin from the beginning. I did nothing to stop her from seeing him. We need to focus our energy on getting Solis through this, not on getting Ronin caught up. Ronin does love her. He's not one of those guys that just likes to mess around with young girls."

"Loves her? I don't care! He's done!"

"Dahlia . . . Why call the police? What good would it do? None. It'll just leave Solis alone to care for a baby. Ronin will take care of her and the baby. He's got the money to do it. We don't. I'll go see him once we know Solis is okay."

"Take care of her? He got her pregnant!"

"Dahlia, I'm telling you . . . don't do it. Solis will never forgive you. If you'd listened to me, we wouldn't be here now."

"Don't blame this on me. You knew."

"If you hadn't called the authorities, Solis wouldn't have felt like she had to keep it a secret to protect him. I would've known sooner. We all would have."

"You don't think he knows?"

"If he did, she wouldn't be here. She'd have had an abortion, or he'd have told us. I know Solis. She didn't tell him. Go see Solis. I'll call Ronin."

Marlon waited until the nurse took Dahlia back before calling. Ronin picked up on the first ring.

"Marlon? She didn't tell me until this morning."

"You son of a bitch! You knew this morning! Solis is in the emergency room at Lake Methodist. We found her on the floor in her room barely conscious this afternoon!" Marlon shouted.

"Lake Methodist! What happened, Marlon? Is she okay?"

"No! She isn't. If you knew she was sick . . . why didn't you bring her home or call me?"

"Solis wanted . . . I should've told you myself. What'd the doctors say?"

"Severe dehydration. She's been admitted."

"How in the hell did she get this sick and no one noticed?"

"She wanted to protect you. And when Solis wants something, she'll get it, even if it means putting herself in the hospital. Solis loves you, and that is the only reason you're talking to me and not the police."

"I don't care about the police. Solis is all that matters. What else did the doctor say?"

"He said he'd seen marathon runners less dehydrated than Solis. She was still unconscious when I left. Dahlia is there now. It's bad, Ronin. It's really bad."

"I'll be there in twenty."

Frantic, Ronin checked for his keys and wallet, and called Tasha. "Tasha, cancel everything on my schedule for the rest of this week. Say nothing to anyone. I'll call you later with instructions. Call the valet and tell them to bring my car around like yesterday."

"Mr. Jackson, is everything okay? Should I call Mrs. Jackson? Or your father?"

"No! Call no one. Forward all calls to my cell phone."

"If Mrs. Jackson calls?"

"Don't answer. Send her to my voice mail."

*****

Ronin opened the curtain. Solis was asleep with an IV in each arm. Her pregnant belly was more obvious with the monitor on it. A feeling of utter helplessness consumed him. He fought back tears.

"Ronin? What are you doing here? You can't be here. Go before anybody sees you. They're going to take you to jail. I should've said something sooner. I should've taken better care of myself. This is all my fault. I don't want you to go to jail." Solis was distraught.

"Solis, I'm not going anywhere." Ronin lowered the bed's railing and sat on its edge. "I don't want you to worry about it anymore. I don't want you to worry about anything anymore. I want you to rest and get well. Promise me you will only focus on getting well."

"I'm afraid I hurt the baby."

"You did no such thing. The baby is fine. It's you the doctor is worried about."

"What am I going to do, Ronin?"

"You're going to rest and take care of yourself."

"No. What am I going to do? I haven't done anything. I haven't been anywhere. I haven't even finished school."

Deep down, a part of him knew this would happen. She would blame him for ruining her life, and he would have no defense to offer. No matter how much responsibility Solis wanted to take for the present situation, in the end, the fault was his.

"Solis listen to me. We weren't equals when this began. I took advantage of your love and your trust. I selfishly thought only about myself. I love you desperately, and I promise, all the things you want in this life, you will have. I swear it. You will finish high school and go to college. You will travel and live abroad. You will learn as many languages as you want. I'll make sure of it. And if you need to do those things without me, I'll understand."

"You didn't take advantage of me. I love you."

"I love you too. Your love and trust mean everything to me. I will not betray them again."

Solis began to nod off. "I'm tired. Will you stay with me awhile?"

"Yes. Rest. I'll be here when you wake up."

Chapter 42

Ronin sat at his desk. He was tired. He'd spent the night in the recliner in Solis's hospital room. This morning she was able to eat and hold food down. Her color was better too. The nurse assured him Solis was well enough for him to leave for a while to attend to business. The list of tasks before him was considerable.

"Ro, it is Saturday afternoon. You better have a good reason for this!" Damien plopped down in a chair.

"It must be serious if we're all here. You look like hell." Malik sat down.

"Damn boy! What is it?" Byron asked impatiently.

"Gentleman, the three of you are here to save my life. Malik, you are going to get me out of my marriage with Ona as quickly as possible and without the need to liquidate all my assets. Damien, you and Dad are going to keep me out of jail."

"Jail? Did I miss something?" Malik asked, perplexed.

"He doesn't know. My numb nuts of a brother here has been boning the nanny," Damien scoffed.

"So what? I got men cheating on their wives with other men, prostitutes, cousins, sisters, you name it. Who cares about a nanny?"

"Solis is seventeen." Ronin waited for his words to sink in.

"Truthfully, that isn't a first for me. I'll admit I'm surprised you'd be in this situation. Then again, very little surprises me anymore."

"Really? Nothing?" Ronin asked. "What if I told you she's five months pregnant?"

Damien jumped out of his chair. "You got her pregnant! You stupid bastard! I'm your brother, and I want to kill you. I can only imagine what her family is thinking. If she had a father, jail would be the least of your worries."

"D, I don't need a lecture right now. I need to get ahead of the shit storm headed my way."

"You don't think this was a trap?" Byron asked.

"A trap? It's bad enough her mother and my wife think she's my whore. And now you think she's a what? Some broad trying to come up. Damn, all of you! Let me tell you who my Solis is: She's the woman lying in a hospital bed at Lake Methodist, suffering from severe dehydration, because, instead of taking care of herself and our baby, she hid in her room with nausea pills and soda to avoid getting caught and to keep me out of jail. That's who she is."

"Oh god, son, that's bad. Is she going to be okay?"

"We think so. If anything happened to her, I couldn't live with myself."

"Live with yourself? Shut the hell up, you selfish bastard. The girl is in the damn hospital . . . and you put her there. I can't believe you're that guy. I told you, you could hurt her." Damien shoved him.

"Gentlemen let us get to the point. Does her family know? Does Ona know?" Malik asked.

"Her family, yes. Ona, no," Ronin answered.

"When does she turn eighteen?"

"In December"

"When is the baby due?"

"In January."

Malik thought for a moment. "I need to get this divorce done before then. Ona is going to come for your life. This is going to be ugly."

"That's why I'm hiring you. You're the best divorce attorney in the county. You're as ruthless as she is."

Damien shook his head. "Ona is the least of your problems. Doctors are mandated reporters. If Officer Stanton was here once, he will be again . . . and soon. But I got it."

"Gentlemen, would you mind giving me a moment with my son."

Damien and Malik left. Byron closed the door behind them.

"Boy, did it ever occur to you what the fallout of this could do to the firm? Clients are going to leave. No one wants to be associated with a pedophile."

"Pedophile? Solis is seventeen, not twelve. I'm not a pedophile. Fuck you for even suggesting it."

Byron came across Ronin's jaw with a left hook, knocking him back into his chair.

"No one is going to give two shits that Solis is seventeen. People don't make those kinds of distinctions. I should've dragged your ass out of that hotel. I didn't think you were dumb enough to get her pregnant!"

Ronin massaged his jaw. "You're throwing punches now? Dad, I'm a grown man—"

"Are you? If I were a younger man, you'd be laid out in a hospital bed, right next to Solis. Get your ass back to that hospital. Malik, Damien, and I will clean up this pile of shit you've made."

"Dad, I'm sorry . . . I really am."

"I'm not the one you need to be apologizing to. Ona, the boys, Solis . . . not me. Pray they forgive you."

*****

"Solis, you're an idiot." Iris sat on the edge of Solis' hospital bed.

"I know. I was afraid. What if something happened to him? I'd never forgive myself." Solis replied.

"You could've died. Marlon is pissed. He knows I knew."

"I'm sorry, Iris. Forgive me. I don't know what I'm going to do." Solis dropped her head in her hands.

"Well, first, you're going to eat this nasty ass Jell-O. Next, we'll make a plan to get you caught up in all your classes. We have the same ones; it shouldn't be hard. We'll keep this whole thing a secret until we can't."

"I'll get caught up, but I'm not going back to school. I'll go on independent study. People will ask who the father is. . . I don't need that."

"What did Ronin say?"

"He says he loves me and is going to take care of me. He says he isn't mad; just upset I didn't tell him sooner. He apologized. I think he's going to divorce his wife. What if she calls the police? Or takes the boys from him? I'll die."

"It's going to be okay, Solis. You're my best friend and the strongest person I know. Ronin is a lawyer, right? He's got lawyer money and lawyer friends. He'll figure it out. Men like him don't go to jail. Trust me."

"I love you, Iris."

"Of course, you do. I'm awesome. I love you too."

Chapter 43

Ona pulled in the driveway just as the as the truck with the last of Ronin's belongings drove away.

"You getting new furniture, Mrs. Jackson?" Christopher asked, opening the door.

"Not that I know of."

Christopher followed Ona inside with her luggage.

"Thank you, Christopher." Ona tipped him and shut the front door. "Ronin. You here?"

"Yes. I'm in the den."

Ona dropped her purse and keys on the couch. She noticed several things were missing from the room. "You pack up a few things while I was gone? I've only been in Atlanta three days."

"Sit down, Ona."

"No, I'd rather stand. Ronin, what's going on?"

"I packed my things and moved them out because I know you aren't going to want me back here after this."

"After what?"

"I want a divorce."

"No."

"Ona, I want a divorce. I cannot stay in this marriage. It isn't fair to you."

"Fair to me! You think divorcing me is fair! Are you an idiot?"

"What do you want me to say? I do not want this. You shouldn't want this."

"What do I want you to say? Try 'I am sorry' and 'I will never do it again.' Or maybe 'I love you and I don't want to destroy our family.'"

"I can't say those things, Ona. I'd be lying to you if I did."

"You son of a bitch! You don't love me anymore? You love her? Her pussy must be good if you are willing to leave your family for her!" Ona screamed.

"Ona, you need to calm down."

Ona slapped him hard. "Don't tell me to calm down! I won't let you do this. I won't let you leave me for her. I won't!"

Ronin stood to leave. "Ona, I'm filing for divorce. You should find an attorney."

"I will not. I love you. You can't leave." Ona grabbed his arm, pulling him back toward the couch.

Ronin didn't move. "Let me go, Ona."

"You're really leaving me for a child! A child!" Ona shrieked, tears streaming down her face.

Ronin removed her hand. "I'm sorry, Ona, but I can't do this. I will get the boys this evening to give you some time to yourself."

"Why? Tell me why. And don't lie to me."

"Solis is pregnant."

"Pregnant! You got her pregnant!"

Ona attacked him, slapping and punching in a frenzy.

Ronin subdued her, doing his best not to hurt her. "Ona, stop. I'm leaving now before this gets out of hand. When I let go, don't hit me again."

"You can't do this to me. I won't let you. Do you hear me? I won't let you. She can't have you!"

Ronin released her. "Goodbye, Ona."

*****

"You and Mom are getting a divorce, aren't you?" Ronin Jr. asked calmly.

"Yes, we are," Ronin answered.

"What does that mean? Are we not going to see you anymore? Where are we going to live?" Robert asked, confused.

"It means that Mommy and Daddy aren't going to be living together anymore. You and your brother will stay in the house with Mommy and sometimes with me at my new house."

"Why? Why are you getting a divorce? Don't you love Mommy?" Robert asked tearfully.

"I love Mommy very much. Sometimes people just need to be apart. Have you ever had a friend at school who you liked a lot but didn't always get along with?"

"Yes," Robert answered in a quiet voice.

"What do you do when that happens?"

"We take a time out and go play with other people."

"Mommy and Daddy are like that—friends who can't be friends right now. Understand?"

"I think so. You're always going to be my daddy, and Mommy will always be my mommy, right?"

"Always," Ronin tried to reassure him.

"I don't want to talk about this anymore. It makes me sad. Can I go now?" Robert asked.

"Sure, buddy, we can talk more about it later."

Ronin watched as Robert left the table and went upstairs. It took everything in him not to breakdown and cry. He knew Robert wouldn't take it well. Ronin Jr. hadn't said a word. And after Ona's reaction, his conscience was kicking his ass. He wasn't doing the right thing for any of them.

"Are you okay, Chief? Talk to me," Ronin asked.

"It sucks. I have friends whose parents are divorced. I get it. I've been talking to them a lot."

"I expect you to be angry with me. It's okay if you are."

"I'm not happy about it. I kind of knew it was going to happen. You and Mom have been fighting a lot, and we've been spending a lot of time with Grandma and Grandpa. I'm mad that you hurt Mom. Robert isn't going to be okay either, I think. I mean, you're basically breaking up our family."

"I am. I wish I could explain to you why I'm doing this, but I can't. I want you and Robert to know that this is not your fault. It's mine."

"I know why. It's because you're in love with Solis."

"How on earth did you come to that conclusion?" Ronin asked, stunned.

"I see the way you look at her. Not like with Mom. You hurt Mom and Robert. You're being a total loser."

"You're right. What about you? I hurt you too."

"Yeah, but you aren't going to stay, are you?"

"No, I'm not."

"Just make sure you're around. Some of my friends have dads they never see. Promise you won't be one of those dads. Even after the baby comes."

"Baby?"

"Dad, I know Solis is pregnant. You grown-ups are horrible at keeping secrets. You talk too much."

"Does Robert know?"

"No. I didn't tell him. He wouldn't get it. You should bring Solis back. He misses her a lot. I miss her too."

"We'll see. How do you feel about that? About Solis being pregnant."

"I feel like you're a jerk. I'd say something else, but I'm not allowed to say bad words."

"The word you're searching for is asshole." Ronin smiled.

"Yup." Ronin Jr. laughed.

"You have every right to feel that way. Chief, you'll never have to worry about me being around. Ever. I promise."

"Good. We should go get Robert. He gets super sad if you leave him alone too long."

"You're a very mature young man, Chief. And a better big brother than I was. I'm very proud of you."

"Dad, I'm eleven and a half. I'm not a baby."

"No. No, you aren't."

"Ice cream. Let's take Robert for ice cream. It always cheers him up. And I want a waffle cone. One of those chocolate-dipped ones."

"Waffle cone, coming up."

Chapter 44

"Solis, this onesie is too cute." Dahlia held the up garment.

"I refuse to let you turn this child's life into a bottle of Pepto Bismol. There are other colors, Dahlia." Marlon held up another onesie. "Solis, what do you think? Lilac or Pepto?"

"Baby girls wear pink!" Dahlia shouted back playfully.

"Buy whatever you want. I don't care!" Solis burst into tears and ran from the store. Marlon started to follow, but Dahlia stopped him. "I got this."

Solis sat outside on the edge of the planter box bench. Dahlia joined her.

"Dahlia, most days I feel like I'm fumbling around in the dark. Sometimes I wake up and think it's all a dream, and then reality sets in. I can't do this. What if I resent her? What if I— "

"Treat her like I've treated you? You won't. You don't have it in you. You're the most loving person I know."

"I'm scared. I don't think I'm ready for all of this."

"You aren't. But I know you can do this. We're going to be with you every step of the way. It's okay to be scared. It isn't all on you."

"I love you, Dahlia. I'm sorry I've been so . . . I should've listened to you."

"Solis, you didn't listen to me because I taught you not to. All your life, I've left you on your own. You and Marlon. It's why we're here now. It's why Ronin was able to do what he did."

"I love Ronin. He didn't do anything to me."

"I know you believe that, but even he knows that's not true. But what's done is done."

"I'm tired. Can we go home?"

"Yes. I'll go get the car while Marlon checks out."

"Already done." Marlon held up several shopping bags.

"Good. Did you get validation?" Dahlia asked.

Marlon handed Dahlia the receipt and sat down.

"Solis, you need to rest more. You haven't recovered from your sickness. It took a lot out of you."

"I do rest."

"Solis, most nights I find you asleep with your face in a book."

"I have to focus on finishing school. At the rate I'm going and with the credits I already have, I should have my diploma in December, before Gypsy gets here. That way, I can take next semester off and walk with my class in the spring."

"I can't believe you're going to name that baby Gypsy."

"Gypsy Marlonia Jackson."

"You're naming her after me?"

"Don't cry you, big baby. You've been my rock my whole life. Why shouldn't my gem have your name?"

"That's the most amazing thing anyone has ever done for me, and I will love you forever for it."

"I love you too. Now the most amazing thing you can do for me is rub my feet."

Chapter 45

"The district attorney isn't going to press charges," Damien announced.

"Are you for real?" Ronin asked, surprised.

"If the victim of a crime won't admit they're a victim and the evidence is still two months away, it's kind of hard to make a case. Factor in that she'll be eighteen by the time the evidence shows up . . . there really is no point in pursuing the case any further. But believe me, the DA wasn't happy about it. You're welcome."

"Yeah, you should thank him. Now we can focus on Ona," Malik dropped a legal folder on the desk. "I sent the last settlement offer to her attorney, Donald Spencer. He's a good guy. He knows our offer is more than fair. I think he can get her to settle. She wants full custody. He knows even if we go to trial, she isn't going to get it. After the mediator's report and the DA's decision, Solis is no longer an issue. I told Donald we couldn't meet face-to-face. Ona is crazy. You should hear the messages she leaves on my phone. I'm not sure if the boys don't need to be with you, at least until she can get it together. I told Donald as much. He can't say anything, but I know he understands me."

Ronin flipped through the settlement offer. "I knew Ona would be angry and hurt. I didn't expect her to go off the deep end like this. The boys seem okay for now. The moment I think otherwise, you know what to do."

"Good afternoon, gentlemen." Audra came in the office.

"Mom, what are you doing here?" Ronin asked, kissing Audra on the cheek.

"Do I need a reason?" she replied. "Malik, would you and Damien excuse us? Ronin and I need to talk."

Audra gave Malik and Damien a look making it clear she wanted them to leave. They did.

"Ronin, Ona is hurting. You should be more understanding."

"Mom, I would be if she wasn't hell bent on trying to convince me to call off the divorce. Where's Solis? Shouldn't she be with you today?"

"She is asleep. She refused lie down in a bed but agreed to sit in your father's recliner. She was gone in minutes. That girl is more stubborn than a mule. The poor thing is tired. Her obsession with finishing school is taking a toll on her. She is driven. An admirable quality. Not so much when you are eight months pregnant."

"She's growing on you. I can see it. I knew you wouldn't be able to hold out for long." Ronin smiled.

"I will admit she has grown on me. You need to talk with her about coming to live with us. It is ridiculous, this back and forth. She is too pregnant for that."

"Mom, she likes being at home with her family. She's comfortable there."

"She needs supervision. She still isn't well. I went to her last appointment. She is anemic and not gaining weight like she should, which means she isn't eating well. Marlon and Dahlia aren't home enough. Talk to her."

"Okay. I'll try."

"Try hard. Every time I see Solis, I'm reminded of how disappointed I am in you. You are a lot like your father. Both of you have a weakness for beautiful women, but Solis is not a woman. She is a girl. An amazingly mature girl, but a girl, nonetheless. You knew better. You know better. I may not have been fond of Ona, but you were wrong. Your father hasn't always been faithful, but at least he had enough respect for me not to rub my face in it. You're lucky Solis is who she is, or you would be in a world of hurt."

"Mom, I know . . ."

"Do you? Do you men ever know? All of you fumble around with your dicks in your hands, wreaking havoc on the world."

"Our dicks in our hands? Who are you, and what've you done with my mother?"

"That girl loves you. Truly loves you. It is unusual that a girl that young would know what real love is, but she does. I can see it whenever she looks at you. That child almost killed herself to protect you. You didn't deserve it. You don't deserve her. You should be in jail." Audra was shaking.

Ronin was floored. Audra Jackson always kept her composure. Today she let the veil drop.

"Mom, I know I should—"

"Save it. I don't want to hear it. It is Solis' forgiveness you should be begging for, not mine. I am your mother. I will love you regardless."

"You've every right to be disappointed in me. I'm disappointed in myself. Mom, I love her. I will take care of her and our child. You know I will."

"Good. You can start right now. Go talk to her. Tell her she is staying with us."

"Now?"

"Yes, Ronin Byron Jackson, now."

"I have meetings."

"Damien and your father have meetings. You have a baby due in six weeks, which really means any day now. Go!"

Ronin passed by his father on his way out. "Mom is here. I may not be back today."

Byron laughed. "Sounds like it. I'll talk to Tasha. Mrs. Jackson, would you join me?"

Audra waited until Ronin was on the elevator before joining Byron.

"Don't you think you were a little harsh? Jail? You and I both know that would've served no purpose. If he went to jail, how the hell would he be able to take care of Solis, the baby, and the boys? He loves her, Audra. He'll do right by her. I'll see to it."

"Harsh? I wasn't harsh enough. Jail? The only reason he isn't in jail now is because you know Charles, not because of Damien. Any other district attorney would have pressed charges. You knew about this. You knew, and you did nothing."

"Woman, Ronin is a grown man. What was I supposed to do? I talked to him. Father to son. Man, to man. Like any fool in love, he wouldn't see reason. Solis is the one. Sixteen, seventeen, or not. She's the one. You, me and the rest of the world are just going to have to get over it."

Audra turned her back to him. Forty-one years, they'd been married. It seemed like forever ago that she stood at the altar taking her vows. Byron was twenty-eight. She was eighteen. Six months later, Ronin was born.

Byron turned her around. "Audra Jackson, I know I haven't always done right by you. Like you said, I was one of those men running around with my dick in my hand, wreaking havoc on the world. You stuck with me even though I didn't deserve it. You are one of the strongest women I have ever met. I love you."

"One of them?" Audra gave him a jokingly perturbed look.

"Yes. The other one is in love with our son."

Chapter 46

"No! Absolutely not!" Ona screamed.

"Ona, this settlement is a good one. Ronin has agreed to your visitation schedule. He'll continue to pay the mortgage and the school tuition in lieu of child support. You and the boys can stay in the house. When they leave for college, you can sell it and split the proceeds or put it in a trust for the boys. He's also offered to pay you for 25 percent of my services. We can fight it out. I'd be lying if I told you I thought that was the better option."

"The son of a bitch knocked up a teenage girl, and you're telling me that a judge won't give me sole custody?"

"However inappropriate their relationship may be, the district attorney is not pressing charges, a fact that doesn't help our case. The mediator's report isn't any better. It stopped short of recommending the boys be with Ronin; but did mention concerns about your mental fitness."

"I read that stupid report. The mediator was biased."

"Biased or not, it is what it is. She found that the boys were handling the separation well and attributed a lot of that to Solis. You, on the other hand, were not. Frankly, Ona, I'm concerned too. You have an unhealthy fixation with this girl. As your attorney, I'd advise you to take this offer. Save your money and use it for a good therapist. If you don't, you could end up losing the custody you have."

"It's not fair! It's just not fair! She gets him and my sons. Do you know it's a girl? A girl! Ronin always wanted a girl, and now she's giving him one."

"Nothing in divorce is fair. It is a terrible thing for everyone involved. I wish I could tell you different. I've been doing this for a long time."

Joi held Ona's hand. "Ona, you should listen to him. I've been down this road before. After months of negotiation and a two-week trial, I didn't get half of what Ronin is offering. I think Ronin deserves to burn in hell too; but you don't need to burn with him. Take the offer."

Ona still could not believe Ronin was leaving her. She hadn't seen him since the day he packed his bags and left. Byron and Audra were always the ones to pick up or drop off the boys. All discussions about the divorce settlement were done through their attorneys. When they did talk, it was only to discuss the boys and logistics, nothing more. The boys were her only source of information. Ronin Jr. was tight-lipped, but Robert would go on and on until Ronin Jr. stopped him. That's how she found out the baby was a girl. She was broken inside.

"If I accept this settlement offer, how soon will the divorce be final?"

"Since you both have agreed to everything, it only requires a judge's signature. Two weeks. Four at the most."

"Where do I sign?"

"I'll prepare the papers for your signature. Can you come back, say, Friday?"

"Yes. I'll see you then."

"I am truly sorry, Ona. I really am."

"Thank you, Donald." Ona left the room.

Donald held Joi back. "Joi, I'm worried about her. See if you can get her to see a therapist or something."

"I know. I know. I am too. I am trying. Believe me, I am."

*****

Joi selected the lobby on the elevator panel. She waited for the doors to close before she spoke.

"Ona, I'm worried about you. Maybe you need to take a vacation. Get away. You could use the down time to see a counselor. I'll call my therapist. She's pretty good. I think you'll like her. If you want, the boys can stay with me . . . not Ronin."

"He took ten years of my life. And now he's trying to buy me off. That's what that settlement is. He's trying to make himself feel better by being generous. It's insulting."

"Yes, it is. But if he wants to fall on his sword. Take the money and run."

"Joi, I am the woman whose husband left her for the teenage nanny. Do you know how humiliating that is? He was sleeping with her right under my nose, and I didn't see it. My sons adore little Ms. Mary Poppins. She's having his baby for Christ's sake."

"Ona, men leave their wives every day for younger women. The fact that Ronin left for a teenage girl doesn't make you any less of a woman. If anything, it makes him less of a man."

"It's her fault. She could have said no. She lied to me. You don't know Solis like I do. There was no seduction. It was her plan all along."

"I doubt it. I know you don't want to hear that. Ronin seduced a sixteen-year-old girl, kept her as his mistress, and got her pregnant. Hell, you told me yourself she was a virgin—a fact the son of a bitch rubbed in your face. Ronin is not the man you married. He has changed."

The elevator opened on the lobby.

"Great. The coffee stand is still open. You want anything?" Joi asked.

"Sure, get whatever. I need to go to the ladies' room. I'll be right back."

For the first time since this whole thing began, Joi was frightened for her sister. The only person she could think to call for help was Charlotte. She dialed quickly, hoping she'd pick up before Ona got back.

"Joi, baby, I'm so glad you called. How's Ona? She doesn't say much when I call."

"Mom, you need to come—now. Ona is not okay. Not by a long shot."

"I'll be there as soon as I can. I'll call you as soon as I find a flight."

"Good. I have to go. Ona will be back. See you soon."

Joi put the phone down just as Ona made it back to the lobby. "I didn't order. Ona, are you okay? You don't—"

"I'm fine. I just need to sit down for a minute."

"Ona, are you high?"

"No. Just a little Xanax."

"Your doctor told you to take those at night. You're taking them during the day now?"

"I need them during the day too. Without them, the pain is overwhelming. I can't function."

"Ona, this is bad. You need to see someone today. Today."

"She has my life."

"No. You do. Xanax isn't going to bring Ronin back or make that baby go away. It will make you lose custody of the boys . . . or worse. I understand the pain you are feeling more than you know. Ronin was wrong for what he did. But you got to pull it together."

"You're right, Joi. I'll go see someone. . . today."

Chapter 47

The doorbell rang. "I'll get it," Solis called out.

"No, you won't. Sit down. I'll get it," Audra scolded her.

Before Audra could get to the door, Ona was standing in the hallway.

"You planned this. You got pregnant on purpose. Ronin is only with you because you trapped him." Ona spat her words out in a low hiss.

"Ona, I know you're hurt," Solis replied.

"You have no idea how I feel! You took my husband from me! You lied to my face! I invited you into my home! I allowed you into the lives of my children! You stole from me! You stole my life from me!"

"Ona, the boys love and adore you. You're their mother. Nothing will change that. You still have your life. You can do anything you want."

"Anything I want? I want my husband back, you whore!"

Audra stood in front of Solis. "Ona, you need to leave this girl alone. What Ronin did to you was wrong, and I told him so. I have been where you are. I understand, I truly do, but this must stop. It is over."

"Byron didn't leave you."

"He did not. But if he had, I would not be standing in his mother's house making a fool of myself."

"You hated me. Hated me. His wife. But you'll defend his whore?"

Audra opened the door. "Solis is not his whore. And you are not his wife. Now please have some self-respect Ona and don't make me throw you out of my house."

*****

Ona slammed her bedroom door. She caught a glimpse of her reflection in the mirrored closet doors. The woman staring back at her was defeated, a shell of her former self.

She hurled the vanity bench at the closet doors. Her image shattered, leaving the floor covered in broken glass and the doors off their hinges.

Ona noticed a box far back on a high shelf. She stepped in the closet and pulled it down. There was a key taped to the bottom. She opened the box. A .38-caliber revolver stared back at her.

Her phone rang. It was Charlotte. Ona set the box down, never taking her eyes off the gun.

"Mom," Ona answered.

"Ona, you sound upset. Are you okay?"

"You just caught me at a bad time."

"Are the boys with you? I'd love to talk to them."

"No. They're with Joi. You should call there. The boys would be glad to hear from you."

"I will. I was calling to tell you that I'm coming to visit. I'll be there Friday. Maybe we can take the boys out?"

"Sure. Do you need a ride from the airport? When does your flight come in?"

"Friday at six. Ona, baby, are you okay? You don't sound like yourself. Maybe you should call Joi?"

"Mom, I'm fine. I'll see you Friday."

"Ona, I love you."

"I love you too, Mom."

Chapter 48

Ronin heard a gentle knock on the door. "Come in, Tasha, you know you don't have to knock."

"That'd be true if I were Tasha." Solis giggled.

"Solis, what are you doing here?"

"I'm here to see you."

"How'd you get here?"

"I drove that expensive car you bought me."

"Alone? Audra let you out of the house?"

"Yes, I'm not a prisoner, you know."

"No, you aren't. You're nine months pregnant. You could go into labor at any moment."

"Don't remind me. I had a run in with Ona this morning."

"What? Where? Are you okay?"

"At the house. I think Audra set her straight."

"I have to talk to her. You don't need the stress."

"Enough about her. I came here to see you. I was thinking we could . . . I don't know?"

"I can't imagine you'd want to."

"I've wanted to for three weeks. Since you couldn't imagine I'd want it, I figured I'd take the initiative. Besides, I read that it can make the baby come faster. And I'm all for that."

"All you had to do was ask."

"There was a time I didn't have to ask."

"I was simply trying to be . . . I figured, by now, you'd be too uncomfortable. I was trying to be a gentleman."

"Gentleman are for ladies. I'm not feeling all that ladylike. Tonight?"

"Well, since you took the initiative and came all this way . . . how about now?" Ronin drew Solis in close. "I've missed you."

"I've missed you too."

"Mrs. Jackson! Mr. Jackson isn't expecting you. You can't just go in . . ."

Tasha tried in vain to keep Ona out of the office, but Ona shoved her aside.

"Ronin, I want to talk to you." Ona demanded.

"I'm sorry, Mr. Jackson. I tried to keep her out. She wouldn't listen," Tasha cried frantic.

"It's okay, Tasha. I understand. I'll take it from here."

Ronin could see something was terribly wrong. Ona was disheveled. Her eyes had the look of a trapped or wounded animal. He knew he needed to get control of the situation and fast.

Ronin lifted Solis off the desk and gently placed her feet on the floor.

"Solis, I want you to leave now. Tasha, please take Solis with you."

"On your desk? She's a good little whore, isn't she? Don't you see, Ronin, that's all she is? There's no reason for us to end over her. I don't care about the baby. We can work this out. Just leave her!"

"Solis, Tasha, go now. Ona and I need to talk."

"Don't move," Ona said with a deadly calm.

"Ronin, she has a gun! Ronin!" Solis screamed.

Ronin slowly raised his hands, "Ona, relax. Think about what you're doing."

"Now do I have your attention? All I wanted you to do was listen. All I wanted you to do was leave her. You wouldn't. Why did you bring her into our lives? I told you she couldn't have you. I told you I wouldn't let her have you."

"You have my attention. Ona put the gun down before you hurt someone."

"Hurt someone? What would you know about hurt? Tell me. What would you know?" Ona shouted, the gun shaking in her hand.

"I'm calling the police." Tasha ran to the door.

Ona turned to follow her, and the gun went off.

"Ronin," Solis whispered. Blood trickled from her mouth.

"No! Oh god, no! No! No! Solis, baby, no!"

Ronin jumped over the desk in time to catch Solis before she hit the floor.

"Tasha, call 911! Solis, baby, baby, stay with me. Stay with me."

Tasha grabbed the desk phone. Ona stood completely still, the gun in her hand. Damien came in from down the hall.

"Holy shit! Ona, what the fuck did you do?" Damien took the gun from her hand. "Ronin! Ronin! Is she breathing?"

Ronin put his ear to Solis' mouth. "Yes."

"You got to get her to the lobby. It'll be faster than waiting for the paramedics to get up here. Carry her. Take the stairs."

"Oh god, Damien, if she—"

"Go, goddamn it! Go!"

Damien helped Ronin take Solis to the stairs. They were four floors up, and Ronin took the stairs two and three at a time. He could feel Gypsy moving. Solis' water had broken and was running down her legs; there was blood everywhere.

The paramedics were coming into the lobby when Ronin made it to the ground floor.

"Over here! Over here!" Ronin screamed.

The paramedics placed Solis on the gurney and ran to the ambulance, working as they went. Ronin held Solis' hand; he could see the fear in her eyes, and it hollowed him. Solis' belly exposed; Ronin could see Gypsy moving vigorously. Solis' eyes closed, and her hand went limp.

"Stay with me, Solis. Why can't you move faster?"

"Sir, I need you back off. If you don't, I can't help her." The medic moved Ronin back.

Ronin was beside himself. It seemed like forever when they finally reached the hospital. Ronin listened as the paramedics rattled off Solis' vitals. They weren't good. A crushing pain filled his chest; he could barely breathe.

A nurse came out to get him. "Sir, we need some information. Please come with me."

Chapter 49

"Tasha, is it? I'm Officer Paris. Tasha, can you tell us what happened?"

"She shot her! She pushed past me. I couldn't stop her. I didn't know she had a gun. Ona was screaming at him. I ran to call the police, and she shot her. Oh god, the baby!"

Officer Paris turned to Damien. "Sir, can you tell me what you witnessed?"

"I heard the gun shot from down the hall. When I got here, Ona was standing there with a gun. Solis was on the floor in Ronin's arms. I took the gun from Ona, helped Ronin get Solis downstairs to the paramedics, secured the gun, and waited for you to arrive."

Officer Paris closed his notepad. "Thank you both. I know this is hard. Don't go too far, we may have more questions."

Ona hadn't said a word since the gun went off. Damien moved toward her. Officer Paris stopped him. "Sir, you can't—"

"You crazy bitch! You better pray she doesn't die. You better pray their baby doesn't die. Ronin will kill you. He's going to kill you for this, and there is nothing these men can do to save you."

Officer Paris placed his hand on Damien's chest. "Sir, I am going to have to ask you to leave now."

"Damien." Tasha touched his face. "We need to go. Ronin needs you. We need to call your father."

Damien took his phone out of his pocket. The blood on his fingers obscured the phone's touch recognition, forcing him to wipe his hands on his shirt. Distracted by the blood on his hands and clothing, Damien didn't hear his father answer the phone.

"Hello? Hello? Damien?" Byron called out.

"Dad . . ." Damien held the phone, unable to speak; adrenaline waning, shock was setting in.

"Damien, what's wrong?"

"She shot her. There's so much blood . . . so much. She won't survive. Ronin . . ."

"Damien, son . . . Who got shot? Where are you?"

"Dad, Ona shot Solis."

"What? Where are you? Where's Ronin? Solis? Damien, talk to me."

"Ronin went to the hospital with Solis. Tasha and I are heading there now. Dad, I . . ."

"Where did they take her?"

"Lake Methodist."

"Son get to the hospital. Call me when you get there. I'll be there as soon as I can."

"Her family? The boys?"

"I'll worry about that. You just get there. Hold it together for your brother's sake. Bye."

Damien hung up the phone. "Tasha, I need to wash my hands."

*****

"Audra. Audra, I need you."

Audra wandered into the family room. "I am going to pick the boys up from school. You want to come?"

"Call Alice and have her pick up the boys when she gets Michael and Brodie Jr. She'll need to hold on to them for a while. I'm not sure how long."

"Is the baby coming? I can't wait. A little girl, after all these years with nothing but you men around."

"Sit down, Audra."

"Why? Byron, what is wrong?"

"Audra Lucille, I need you to sit down. Please. I can't tell you until you sit down."

Byron offered his hand. They both took a seat at the table.

"Audra, Ona shot Solis. She is at Lake Methodist. From the sound of Damien's voice, it doesn't look good."

"She just left here! Ona was standing in my living room not an hour ago! Take me there right now! Right now!"

"Audra, you need to call Alice. Don't tell her the details. Just say the baby is coming, and we can't reach Ona. I'll call Dahlia and Marlon."

"We need to call Ronin."

"No, Damien is on his way. He's going to call me as soon as he gets here."

"Byron, what if—?"

"No, what if. Our son, Solis, our grandchildren, Dahlia, Marlon—they're all going to need us now. Go. Call Alice."

Byron took a deep breath. He knew what he had to do. He just didn't want to do it. How do you tell a mother that her child has been shot and that she and her unborn child may die?

*****

Solis. Shot. Lake Methodist. Hurry.

Byron's words cut through Marlon's heart like a knife. He held the phone, frozen somewhere between fear and rage.

"Was that a call from Solis? Is the baby coming? I'm so juiced. I'll never admit it, but I'm getting into this grandma thing," Dahlia asked cheerfully.

"Dahlia. Dahlia, we need to go to the hospital."

"Marlon, is everything, okay? Are Solis and the baby okay? Why do you sound like that?"

"Ona shot Solis. She's at Lake Methodist. We need to go."

"Marlon, she shot my baby . . . like with a gun shot her?"

Marlon tried his best to hide the terror and anger welling up inside him, but his tears betrayed him.

"Yes, Dahlia. She shot our Solis."

Dahlia let out an inhuman cry. No words. Just screams. Blood-curdling, deafening screams.

Chapter 50

The numbness inside became panic when the officer put the cuffs on. The police walked her out in front of everyone. Alone in the interrogation room, she could still hear the whispers and feel the stares.

"Mrs. Jackson, I am Detective Robert Cobalt. I'd like to ask you some questions about what happened today. I understand you've been read your rights. I want to make sure you understand that you have the right to an attorney. Would you like an attorney?"

"Not at this time," Ona replied.

"Let's get those cuffs off. Would you like some water? I'll have someone bring some."

"Yes. Thank you."

Detective Cobalt sat in the chair across from Ona. "Tell me what happened. Walk me through it."

"I'm not sure what happened."

"You aren't' sure?"

"I don't know what happened." Dahlia sipped her water, desperately trying to get her hands to stop shaking.

"You don't know. Let's try a different question. Why did you go to your ex-husband's office today?"

"He isn't my ex-husband. We're still married."

"I understand you're divorced. Do you still think you're married?" Cobalt asked, confused.

"We're going to work it out."

"Is that why you went to your ex-husband's office today? To work things out?"

"I wanted to talk to him."

"Then why'd you bring a gun?"

"I was in my room, and then I was in his office. Ronin was holding her. Tasha ran for the door. There was a loud bang."

"Ronin was holding who? Who was he holding?"

"I heard screaming. Ronin was screaming."

"You heard a loud bang, and then what happened? Why was Ronin screaming?"

"I don't know. I don't know."

"I think you know. You killed Solis and her unborn child."

"I don't believe you."

"Why'd you kill her?"

"Stop saying that!"

"You shot her in the chest with a .38-caliber revolver. You wanted her dead, and now she is. Where'd you get the gun?"

"I didn't kill her. I just want Ronin to leave her and come home."

"You want him to come home? The man divorced you. Another woman is having his baby."

"Yes. That's what I went there to talk to him about—coming home. I told him I didn't care about the baby. I just wanted him to come home."

"I think you went there to kill your ex-husband because he left you. I think Solis was there, and you shot her instead."

"I'd never hurt my husband."

"Ex-husband. What about Solis? Would you hurt Solis?"

"I . . . I think I want a lawyer."

"You shot a defenseless pregnant woman. Yes, you're going to need a lawyer, Mrs. Jackson. A good one."

Chapter 51

Byron scanned the surgery waiting area. Dahlia's eyes, vacant and empty, watched the surgery suite doors, anxiously awaiting any news. Marlon stared into the distance, a violent storm brewing in his eyes. Ronin, still covered in Solis's blood, sat on the floor, head hung in despair; Audra and Tasha trying to console him. Damien stood next to him, sending updates to other family and friends.

"It's been too long. I don't think she's going to make it," Byron said soberly.

"Dad, Ronin won't survive if Solis and Gypsy die. There's no getting over this."

"I'm more worried about Dahlia, to lose your only child and grandchild to murder. Marlon is a strong young man but carrying a woman through that is a heavy lift."

"Ronin told me that Marlon and Solis were close. She was everything to him."

Doctor Greiner came into the waiting area.

"Is she okay? Are they okay?" Ronin asked, frantically jumping to his feet.

Doctor Greiner addressed the room. "I need everyone to sit down."

"No. Tell me. How is she?" Ronin demanded.

"Mr. Jackson, please sit down," Doctor Greiner asked again, more sternly this time.

Damien touched Ronin's shoulder. "Come on, Ronin, sit down, hear what the doctor has to say."

"You have a baby girl, eight pounds eight ounces. Gypsy is healthy and doing well. The bullet missed her completely. I have her in the NICU as a precaution. You can see her anytime you like."

"What about Solis?" Ronin asked, terrified.

"Mr. Jackson, I'll be honest with you. I'm surprised Solis and the baby made it to the hospital alive."

"Is she going to die?" Dahlia's voice shook.

"Ms. Scott, the surgeons are doing everything they can. The bullet hit her spleen. Right now, she's losing blood as fast as they can give it to her."

"Doctor, what does that mean? Do they have enough blood for her? I don't understand," Marlon asked, confused.

"It means Solis is a fighter. She made it this far. All we can do is hope for the best. Doctor Thornton will update you when she is out of surgery."

Doctor Greiner turned to leave. Byron followed her.

"Doctor Greiner . . ." Byron paused. "Be honest with me."

"I'm not Solis' surgeon, Mr. Jackson, but it doesn't look good. I'm sorry. I truly am."

Byron stepped into an alcove to be sure no one saw his tears. "Dear God, why?"

*****

Dahlia was the first one to the NICU. She wasn't prepared for the flood of emotions that came when the nurse placed Gypsy in her arms. Gypsy was a good mix of Solis and Ronin. Her eyes were all Solis. She hadn't closed them once since the nurse put her in her arms. Dahlia sat in the rocking chair and talked to her.

"Gypsy, my name is Dahlia. I'm your grandma. I want you to know that you have the most amazing mother in the whole world. I'm going to make you a promise. I will always love you like your mother loved me. I'll be the best grandma I can be and better than that if you need me to. I'll even let you call me Grandma. But if you could come up with something else, I'd appreciate it."

"How about Nana Dahlia? Her brothers call me Nana."

"Nana Dahlia. I like the sound of that. Would you like to hold her?" Dahlia offered Gypsy to Audra.

"Oh yes. Yes, please," Audra replied. She took Gypsy in her arms.

"You are the most beautiful baby I have ever seen. Dahlia, you see the way she looks at you? So alert. I have a feeling she is going to be as stubborn as her mother." Audra laughed through her tears.

"If she is, we're all in trouble." Dahlia laughed.

"Dahlia, I am so sorry. I am so sorry. I know there is nothing I can do or say."

"Audra, until I came in this room, everything in me wanted to die. It hurts so bad. If I let my mind go there, even for a moment, the pain is more than I can take. I don't know what to do. I can't imagine my life without her."

Audra hugged Dahlia, Gypsy between them. "We will get through this. Together. You will not be alone. I promise."

Marlon appeared in the doorway. "Is that her? Is that little Gypsy?"

"Gypsy, this is your cousin Marlon." Audra handed her to him.

"She has Solis' eyes. Dahlia, she is beautiful. I just wish—" Marlon stopped, overcome. "I just wish she could see her mother. This should be Solis' moment. Ronin's moment. I . . ." Marlon laid Gypsy down in her islet. "Solis has to pull through this. Gypsy can't . . . I'm going back to surgery waiting."

"Marlon, I'll go with you. I need to check on Ronin. Dahlia, Marlon and I will come for you if anything changes."

As Audra and Marlon left, Dahlia put Gypsy back in her arms. "They just don't know, you're all that's left."

Chapter 52

Dahlia sat on Solis' bed. Sunlight bathed the room in warmth. There were boxes everywhere. She never got to finish packing. Dahlia chuckled to herself. Both Ronin and Marlon told her she couldn't take any of her old furniture with her. Ronin promised he would buy her new replicas. Solis argued that replicas were replicas and, therefore, not authentic. She lost the argument. Eight months pregnant, she couldn't move the furniture herself, and Marlon and Ronin refused to move it.

"Dahlia? The limo is here."

"Marlon, she's gone. My baby girl is gone."

Marlon sat down on the bed next to her. "If you're not ready, Dahlia, I can send the limo away."

"It isn't fair. It should've been me. I didn't want the things she wanted. I couldn't even have imagined them. Yet here I sit, alive, and my baby is dead." Dahlia buried her face in Marlon's chest.

"You've always taken care of both of us, Dahlia . . . always."

"I failed. She was my everything . . . I was supposed to protect her."

"You tried, and I didn't help you. It doesn't seem real. I can't feel anything. I just keep waiting for her to walk through the door."

"I envy you. I feel everything. I know she isn't coming . . . and it's killing me."

*****

The small chapel was filled with yellow roses, the end of each pew adorned with white sateen ribbons and sprays of jasmine and ivy. A white rose petal-covered carpet led the mourners down the aisle to an alter draped in ruby red roses. Solis, beautiful in white, lay at rest in an endless garden of flowers.

Ronin brushed a hair from Solis' face.

"Wake up! Please god, wake up! Tell me this is just a nightmare! Please open your eyes. Please. I'm begging you."

"Ronin." Damien whispered quietly.

"It should be me. Why didn't that bitch kill me?"

"Man, Ro, I have no answers for you. None. It's wrong what happened to her. Wrong."

"She should've killed you! This is all your fault. Solis is dead because of you! I hate you!" Iris sobbed.

"Oh god, this is really happening," Dahlia wailed.

"I'm sorry. I'm sorry," Ronin cried.

Damien could feel the situation getting out of control. Ronin was on the verge of another breakdown. Dahlia was in hysterics. He knew neither of them should be there. They weren't ready.

"We should all step outside and get some air."

Damien began guiding them all toward the door. Marlon followed with Iris and her mother.

Outside, Ronin and Dahlia sat together on a granite bench in the cemetery garden, the silence of grief between them. Dahlia was the first to find her voice in the quiet.

"Solis was the only good thing I'd ever done in this life, and you took her from me. You had no right. She is dead because of you. I hate you. Right now, I hate you with all that is in me, Ronin Jackson. But Solis loved you. She loved you. Gypsy, Gypsy is going to love you. You don't deserve their love any more than you deserve my forgiveness. But for Gypsy's sake and Solis' memory . . . I'm going to forgive you. I wasn't a good mother to Solis. Promise me, you'll be a good father to Gypsy."

"I'm sorry, Dahlia—"

"Don't apologize to me! I don't want your apology, it means nothing. I want your word. Swear it. Swear to me you will be a good father to Gypsy."

"With my dying breath. I will. I swear it."

"I have something for you. Solis kept journals and letters. I found this in her room. It had your name on it."

Dahlia handed Ronin a folded piece of paper and left.

Ronin opened the note, unsure if he should read it.

Dear Diary,

> *Ronin came back into the boutique today. I've been dreaming about him day and night since we met. I don't want to say I was expecting him, but I was. There is just something about him. He seems so lost . . . lonely really. I feel like he was looking for me. Something inside tells me to love this man. To give him my whole heart. It's as if it already belonged to him in some other life, and I'm just returning it. Who knows? Maybe I'm just a silly girl in love with love. Or maybe I've read too many romance novels. I can't explain it. I'm just going to love him. I can feel it.*

"It was my heart that belonged to you. I swear to you on my worthless life, I will never give my heart to another. Not in this life or the next."

Ronin folded the diary page and wept.

Chapter 53

"All rise. The Honorable Judge Thomas Rego presiding." The bailiff spoke in a loud commanding tone.

"Be seated." The judge took his seat on the bench.

"Your Honor, District Attorney Charles Jamison for the state."

"Your Honor, Robert Liba for the defense. My client, Mrs. Ona Claire Hilliard-Jackson, is present."

The judge turned to the clerk. "Please read the charges."

Ona stopped listening at that point. It was a struggle to breathe. Lady Justice was seated on her throne behind the judge. Ona wished she could see behind the blindfold, plead her case; as a woman, maybe she would understand.

"Mrs. Hilliard-Jackson, do you understand the charges against you?" Judge Rego asked.

The truth was she didn't understand any of it. For her, it was surreal nightmare from which she could not wake up. She'd spent every day since her arrest in cages, locked in chains, surrounded by empty women fumbling in the darkness, too blind to see the light. She watched in horror as the strong wept, the weak died, and the dead walked; all the time wondering if that would be her fate. If that wasn't enough, Solis' face and the sound of Ronin's desperate cries kept her awake at night.

"Yes, I understand," she answered.

"Mrs. Hilliard-Jackson, do you understand the charges against you? Has your attorney explained them to you?" the judge asked again.

"I understand, and he has."

"How do you plead?"

She was guilty. The gun was in her hand. She pulled the trigger. She never intended to kill anyone, not Ronin and certainly not Solis or her baby. She was relieved to find out the baby lived.

"Mrs. Hilliard-Jackson, how do you plead?" the judge asked again as if she had not heard him.

"Not guilty. I plead not guilty."

The courtroom was packed, a real media circus. Why not? The story had everything: a cheating husband, a jilted wife, and a pregnant teenage mistress. Just add a murder trial and stir. It was in the papers every day. Every detail of their lives laid bare for the world to see.

Ona couldn't help but think about the boys and how they were handling all this. She felt better when Joi told her Ronin had taken them and moved far enough away to keep them out of the spotlight. He was also allowing her parents to see the boys. She suspected that had a lot more to do with Audra than Ronin.

Joi visited regularly. She kept her supplied with all the comforts of home allowed and more importantly with hope. They hadn't talked about it, but she knew Joi was angry. The charity had suffered since her arrest. No one wanted to give money to a charity for children run by a woman on trial for shooting a pregnant teenage girl. It didn't matter that Joi had nothing to do with it. Everything and everyone she'd ever touched was tainted.

Her attorney was cautiously optimistic that with a change of venue and an argument of extreme emotional distress, they had some hope of a good outcome at trial. The district attorney offered a deal of twenty-five years to life because of what he called the heinous and callous nature of the crime. They turned it down. Twenty-five years to life wasn't a deal. Her attorney told her she needed to prepare herself for the possibility that she could spend a substantial number of years in prison if convicted, even with a sentencing recommendation. The hope was to put on a strong-enough case to get the jury to convict on a lesser charge or force the DA to offer another deal with reduced prison time. At the end of the day, she was going to prison. The only question was, for how long?

Robert Liba was a good attorney. Donald Spencer recommended him. The entire legal community knew Byron and Ronin. Ona was afraid no one would take her case. The cost of mounting her defense was going to be substantial. Ronin, to her disbelief, honored the terms of their divorce settlement. He sold the house and gave Ona's share to her parents. With Robert Liba's agreement to reduce his fees, the additional funds, and her parents help, she would have just enough to defend herself.

Ona glanced over her shoulder. Joi was seated to the left of Charlotte; both smiled when she saw them. Byron and Audra sat behind the district attorney. Byron's face was stone-cold, Audra's expressionless. She could see Dahlia and Marlon seated a few rows back. The anger and hatred in their eyes frightened her. Ronin wasn't there. Ona turned around. Her life was over.

Chapter 54

"Gypsy is four months old, and he still hasn't laid eyes on her." Dahlia sat across the table from Audra holding Gypsy.

"The boys haven't seen him either. Dahlia, I don't know what to do. Damien says most days he has to force Ronin to eat and bathe. Not two nights ago, Damien and Byron had to go searching for him. They found him drunk at her grave site. Damien is afraid to leave him alone. He is convinced it is only a matter of time before he will come home and find him dead."

"I understand his grief, but he made a promise to me. Enough is enough. Audra, pack Gypsy up. We're going to take her to see her father."

"Dahlia, do you think that is wise? Ronin is so unpredictable."

"It's time, Audra. Gypsy needs her father. The boys need their father. Protecting them from his grief isn't helping him any more than it helps them."

"Dahlia, what are you going to do?"

"I'm going to leave Gypsy with her father."

"Dahlia, are you mad? He is in no condition to take care of that child."

"He isn't, and he never will be if we let him languish in the bottom of a bottle drowning his grief. I know what it's like to be in such a dark place that you can't climb out. Do you know what got me through then?

Solis. She never let me languish . . . no matter how hard I tried. Gypsy will do the same. Let's go."

*****

Damien answered the door. "Mom, Dahlia, what are you doing here?"

"We're here to see Ronin." Dahlia stared Damien straight in the eye, daring him to challenge her.

He moved out of the way and let them in. They found Ronin asleep on the couch. Dahlia gave Gypsy to Audra and pushed Ronin off the couch and on to the floor.

"Get up! Get up right now! You're not going to do this anymore. You're going to get your shit together. Right now." Dahlia took Gypsy from Audra and placed her in Ronin's arms. "My daughter died to give you that child. You will take care of her like you promised."

Ronin looked down at Gypsy. She gazed up at him. "She has her eyes. I can't do this. I can't do this. Take her back."

"You can, and you will. You will because Gypsy needs you. You will because Ronin Jr. and Robert need you. If you don't, I'll have Marlon and Damien drag you back home."

"You don't understand. I killed her! I killed her! She is dead because of me. You said it yourself. I was supposed to protect her, and I didn't. Ona killed her because of me. All my children have lost their mothers because of me. Don't you understand? What am I going to tell Gypsy when she grows up? I killed her mother. Take her back. Take her back and leave me alone."

"I will not take her back. Everything you need is in that diaper bag. Come on, Audra. We're leaving."

"What? You can't leave me with her. You have to take her back," Ronin cried.

Dahlia stopped. "Ronin, you made me a promise . . . remember? Remember what you said?"

Gypsy smiled and giggled. For the first time since Solis' death, Ronin could see through the fog of his grief, if only a little. ". . . with my dying breath, I swear it."

Chapter 55

Ronin Jr. stepped through the cemetery gate. He knew exactly where his father was. Ronin was in the same place he had been every Saturday morning for twelve years. He thought about Solis as he made his way through the rows of headstones. Only seventeen when she died, he was older now than she was then.

"Hey, little man. You aren't so little anymore, are you?" the groundskeeper called out to him.

"No, sir," Ronin Jr. answered.

"Well, you know where he is. I've worked here a long time. I can say that I've never seen a man grieve over a woman like that. It's as if he would rather be in the ground with her than walking around amongst the living."

The groundskeeper did not know how true his words were. Grief was his father's constant companion. He often wondered if it always would be.

"Hey, Dad."

"When the hell did you get here? No one told me you were here."

"Dad, I always come home for Thanksgiving. Does anyone need to tell you that?"

"How did midterms go? You make dean's list this semester?"

"Fine and yes. Is Robert still thinking about going to culinary school?"

"Yes, and don't you encourage him. I swear, your grandfather and I started our own firm, hoping the two of you would take over someday.

And what do we get for all our hard work? An English teacher and a chef. Maybe Damien's sons will find their way into law school."

"Where is Gypsy? I brought her something."

"She'll be excited. I think she took your leaving for school harder than any of the rest of us."

"That's because I'm the best big brother ever."

"Don't let Robert hear you say that." Ronin laughed.

"How are Tasha and Damien?"

"Good, they'll be here for Thanksgiving dinner. You won't recognize Little Solis . . . She's gotten so big. She's walking now. Is your grandmother still working on Thanksgiving dinner?"

"You should see it, Dad. Nana, Nana Dahlia, and Robert are all in the kitchen. They couldn't be happier."

Over the years, Dahlia had come to be like a daughter to Audra. For the first time in her life, Dahlia knew a mother's love. Dahlia took to being a grandmother like a duck to water. Byron, affectionately known as Papa, relished his role as grandpa. Between Marlon, Audra, Byron, and Dahlia, he had to fight for time with the kids. No matter how much he complained. Ronin was happy.

"So where is Gypsy?" Ronin Jr. asked again.

"She's out with Marlon."

"That man is crazy, and Gypsy loves every crazy bit of him."

"What twelve-year-old girl wouldn't love a man who liked fashion and shopping as much or more than she does?"

"I saw Mom yesterday. Sometimes I feel like I visit both of you in prison. Dad, it's been years. Solis wouldn't want you here. She wouldn't want you to live like this."

"Son, I pray one day you will know a love like Solis. I miss her so much, it hurts. Every morning I wake up, I have to figure out a way to get through another day without her."

"Dad, there are other women. You're still young."

"Not for me. I'm the reason she is here. Her whole life wasted because of me. Our daughter will never know her mother because of me. I should be here. Not her. I will never forgive myself."

"Dad, Mom is the reason Solis is here. Not you."

"If I hadn't done what I did, none of this would've happened. I wish she had killed me. Death would be a better fate than this."

"Well, she didn't. Maybe you can start living like it. Here, this is for you."

Ronin Jr. handed his father a box wrapped in silver paper with matching ribbon.

"What is it?"

"Open it."

Ronin tore the paper. It was the leather journal Solis bought him for his fortieth birthday.

"Where'd you find this?"

"In a closet. I thought, at fifty-two, you could use a reminder that life is short and not promised. Solis would want you to finish your list. She said as much."

"I remember the day she gave this to me. I promised her she would get to do everything on her list. I lied. She didn't get to do anything on her list."

"That isn't true. I read the inscription."

"Chief, my heart and my life belong to her. I don't expect you to understand. I don't expect anyone to understand. I'm where I want to be."

"Let's go have coffee. We can get the hazelnut one you like. What's it called?"

"Café aux noisettes à la crème."

"You could've just said French coffee."

"No. I couldn't."

Ronin placed a dozen red and yellow roses on Solis' headstone.

"Dad, why red and yellow? You always leave red and yellow."

"Yellow roses say, 'I went to the florist and picked out something special just for you.' Red because classics never go out of style."